SOULS OF ANGELS

SOULS
OF
ANGELS

A NOVEL

THOMAS
EIDSON

RANDOM HOUSE NEW YORK

Published in the United States by Random House, an imprint of The Random House Publishing Group, a division of Random House, Inc., New York.

RANDOM HOUSE and colophon are registered trademarks of Random House, Inc.

LIBRARY OF CONGRESS CATALOGING-IN-PUBLICATION DATA

Eidson, Tom
Souls of angels: a novel/Thomas Eidson.
p.   cm.
ISBN 978-1-4000-6238-6
1. Parent and adult child—Fiction. 2. Mentally ill fathers—Fiction.
3. Fathers and daughters—Fiction. 4. Mexicans—California—Fiction.
5. Landowners—Fiction. 6. Los Angeles (Calif.)—Fiction. 7. Domestic fiction.
I. Title
PS3555.I36S68 2007
813'.54—dc22   2007008238

Printed in the United States of America on acid-free paper
www.atrandom.com

246897531

FIRST EDITION

Book design by Carole Lowenstein

To my wife, Cathy

LOS ANGELES
1882

Only God . . .

Mexican graffiti

scratched into the wall

of a Los Angeles jail

1880s

CHAPTER 1

IT WAS LATE, sometime past three in the morning. She was making her way through the darkness shrouding the old plaza, following the main brick pathway that twisted and turned through overgrown oleanders and scrub oaks and mountains of Castilian roses. The town was silent, the sky deep ebony without a moon, the landscape only faintly illuminated by the glow of the new gas lamps that fringed the hundred-year-old gardens like amber beads on a necklace. Storm clouds were coming in from the north. Somewhere in the distance, a dog howled and a coyote yipped an answer, and she shivered in the cool air and walked faster.

She had been with one of her regular customers and was half drunk and angry because the man had ripped her new dress. She pulled the hem up close to her face and walked on, squinting to see the tear in the material, swearing under her breath. The dress had cost a week's work. She let the material drop and touched gently at the small bruise on her cheek, then stopped and pulled a hand mirror and rouge from her bag and tried to see herself in the moonlight, straightening her hair and patting color over the sore spot. Dorothy Regal was twenty-four years old, though she appeared not over sixteen—the mercy of Providence, she liked to say. She was staring into the glass, wondering how much longer she could sell herself as a child, when something moved in the darkness behind her—her eye just catching a blur of motion in a corner of the little mirror. Her breath reversed in her throat.

"Hello?" she called softly, not wanting an answer.

There was none.

She started walking again, faster and with more purpose, assuring herself that the movement had been made by one of the town's cur dogs hunting garbage left by picnickers. Even so, it wasn't smart being in the plaza this late. Nervous in a way that she didn't fully understand, Dorothy stopped once more, turned in a slow circle, and searched the surrounding blocks of shadows. She could see nothing unusual.

The stars were bright in the sky over the darkened town, the gardens quiet and beautiful, the clouds edging closer. She did not see a figure slipping away through the shadows. But she sensed the movement. For the past month, she'd had this same feeling. She didn't know why. There was just the unease.

Dorothy took a deep breath, then began walking again, drawing her shawl tightly around her. She left the darkness of the plaza and crossed Olive Street, heading north, and turned on to the wide dirt street that was called La Calle del Negro by the Mexicans. Shivering once more, she wrapped her arms around her thin shoulders. She could feel the rainstorm approaching in the cool night air, coming in as it always did during this season from the Tehachapi Mountains to the north, driving the smell of the deserts ahead of it.

Someone was playing a piano badly in one of the few establishments still open, and she could hear weary laughter from a window above her. While she had calmed a bit, she kept moving. She was chilled and tired and wanted sleep.

The road and sidewalks before her were empty. A few lanterns hung outside the buildings, casting dull puddles of yellow light on the ground, and both sides of the street were lined with bars, bagnios, and Chinee caves. Knowing that the Americans ran the liquor and gambling, the Mexicans the bordellos, and the Orientals the opium, she wondered how the place ever came to be called La Calle del Negro.

She stopped in front of a two-story wood-frame boardinghouse, La Fiesta. She was home. At least the room upstairs in the back where she met customers and lived was a home of sorts. She touched again at the bruise on her cheek, a momentary veil of melancholy dropping over her. Maybe she should just go back to her real home. But she shook her head at the thought, hard enough to make her long metal earrings yank at her earlobes. They would never have her back. Anyhow, she didn't know if they were even alive.

The rain was on her quickly, and she pulled her shawl over her head and hurried down the darkened path between two buildings, trotting up the old wooden stairs and entering her room. There was no lock, but she did have a wooden brace that she jammed at an angle between the floor and the doorknob. Finished, she felt better. She pulled her damp dress over her head and laid it out on the small bed. There was dirty wallpaper pasted over the window glass for her customers' privacy, creating a heavy darkness. The rain was pounding hard against the roof. Something about the sound was comforting to her.

Dorothy Regal put her hand on the slight swelling of her belly, held it for a moment, then smiled and struck a match and lit the candle on the nightstand beside her bed. She waited for the small flickering flame to grow before she bent and began to carefully examine the tear in her dress. A moment later, she heard a clicking metallic sound behind her, and she stiffened, then straightened up and slowly turned around. A figure was standing in a dark corner of the room, hatted and dressed in a black wrist-length cape, the hat's brim pulled low over the eyes. Dorothy squinted at what she could see of the features in the weak candlelight. There wasn't much. Her own breath sounded like the wind through the old tree outside her window. And she was trembling.

Dorothy tried to compose herself, reasoning that most of her customers came to her room unannounced and wondering why this one should make her nervous. Her naked shadow lurched awkwardly like a puppet in the flickering candlelight wavering against the wall. Her eyes narrowed again. "It's late," she said.

The figure nodded as if in sympathy and stepped closer. Dorothy was trying to see the face beneath the brim of the hat when something silvery flashed in the dull light like a minnow in a stream. For one brief moment she thought she had been spat on.

Then she was staring up at the ceiling.

CHAPTER 2

SISTER RIA SAT ALONE inside the moving stagecoach, thinking about the dead woman and avoiding the sunlight burning through a crack in the roof, the heat dragging up memories of summers past in this place. But, she told herself for the thousandth time, she was not here for sentimental reasons.

She gazed out the window at a group of Mexican workers stacking orange crates in a small boat on a sandy beach. She hadn't eaten an orange since leaving Saint Augustine's nunnery in Spain, ten years before. Ten years. Could it have been that much time since Spain? It did not seem possible. So much in her life had changed. Not all of it for the best.

Sister Ria of the Benedictine Order of the Sisters of Mercy had been traveling for almost two months from her convent in Poona, India. Days after she had received the cable informing her of the charges against her father, and after the health officials had let her go, she had made her way to the port city of Bombay, where she'd caught a tramp steamer to England. She squirmed on the seat. The very thought of her father made her uneasy. But try as she might, she could not drive away this feeling of anxiety. All she could do was keep reminding herself that she had not come back because of him. She had come for only one reason—to fulfill the promise she had made as a child to her dying mother that she would care for him.

She shook her head at this troubling thought and looked back out at the ocean, puzzling over the unsigned cable that had found her at the tiny hospital outside Poona and left her wondering who had sent it. No one knew where she had disappeared to eleven years ago—no one. She had made certain of that. She shrugged. Obviously, someone knew. Perhaps it had been her older sister, Milagros. But Millie would have signed it. More than likely, it was her father's housekeeper, Aba, who was austerely sober in all she did; it would have been like the old woman not to have included her own name. But how would she have known where to send it?

Sister Ria gave up thinking about the cable and returned to watching the green waves breaking on the long stretch of wet sand, her thoughts playing over the trip she had just made. It seemed to have taken forever. But that was silly, she told herself; the journey had been relatively quick, given the remoteness of Poona and the extreme distances. It had seemed interminable only because she was coming home. And home was the last place on God's good earth she wanted to be.

With barely enough money and food to sustain her, the journey had been difficult. But she had fasted longer and lived in far worse conditions. In the crowded harbor at Liverpool, she had searched until she found a three-mast clipper headed for America and paid her passage by cooking meals on a huge wood-burning stove in the ship's galley. Two weeks ago, she had crossed the American continent, jammed in a Zulu-class compartment of the Union Pacific–Central Pacific railroad. Now she was sweating in the heat inside the mid-week coach from Monterey to Los Angeles, close to her destination.

The stage was rolling down a coastal road, high bluffs to her left, white sand and ocean on the right. It was lonely here. Beautiful but lonely. The Chumash Indians called this stretch of shoreline Mal-ibu—where the surf sounds loud.

Sister Ria stared blindly at the pounding breakers, half listening to the screeching gulls and thinking back to summer days when she and Milagros and their nursemaids had played here. She had loved those days—away from the hacienda, away from him. But those days were gone, and she was no longer a child.

She continued to gaze out at the beach. Then she smiled. Something more important than escaping her father had happened here. She had found God on this very stretch of shore some fifteen years before. She had been thirteen that summer, her life shattered by the deaths of her mother and older brother from smallpox, and by the strange existence she had been forced into living with her father. She tensed. Death seemed to follow her. Elsie—her one friend besides Millie—had died only weeks before that summer day. Sister Ria gripped the edge of the coach seat and watched the waves explode on the sand, forcing herself to stop thinking about death and to remember instead the wondrous thing that had happened in this place.

She had come here with her older sister and their nursemaids to picnic and play in the shallows of the surf. The old man, Manuel Escobar, had followed at a respectful distance on his horse, as he always did whenever they left the hacienda grounds. He had waited on a bluff above the beach, watching them as if they were precious cargo.

The muscles of her body tightened as she recalled the sudden urge that had come over her to walk into the water, to keep on walking, to end this life with her father.

She had waited until the others were eating the noontime meal, then she had waded out into the rolling waves—had been knocked down twice—but kept struggling until she was behind the rising swells of the breakers, her clothing weighing her down in the surging drift of the sea. When the water was up to her neck, the old man had fired his pistol into the air and pointed at her, and hysteria had broken out among the young nurses, who ran up and down the beach, begging her to return.

Her older sister had not begged her. Milagros had understood, had walked down to the edge of the water and watched her—and when she turned around for the last time, Millie had waved goodbye. All these years later, Sister Ria could still see the look of intense concentration on Millie's face. The two of them had a sisters' bond that was wonderfully close. Sister Ria shut her eyes and wiped the tears from her cheeks, remembering the bliss that had descended upon her as she was submerged beneath the sea, drifting at peace in the green waters.

The voice had stopped her.

It had gently called her name. And when she hadn't responded, it had said her name again and seemed to shake her—as if a sea creature had grabbed her—and she'd burst above the water, gasping for air. God had spoken to her. She was absolutely certain of it.

Sister Ria straightened the material of her habit over her knees and gazed out at the surf, remembering the voice, so gentle, so loving, and yet so frightening. "You will serve me" was all it had said. And when she was fourteen, she had tried to serve, paying a freighter to take her in his wagon along with a load of molting chickens to Santa Barbara, dropping her off at the old Franciscan nunnery. She smiled, recalling how the mother superior had said that she, too, looked like a half-plucked chicken, her cape covered in feathers.

The smile left her face. That first try at escaping him had not lasted long. Upon his return to Los Angeles, the freighter had told her father what she had done, and he had come for her. She had tried again a few months later, running away to Guaymas, Mexico, to join a cloistered convent on the coast. But the sisters had said she was too young and had the local priest write to him, and he had sent Aba to bring her home—back to the humiliation that was her life with him.

She had promised the old servant woman that she would not leave again before she came of age—would not try as long as he left her alone, as long as he no longer humiliated her. She had almost kept that promise. But he could not control himself. He could not. And so, three years later, at seventeen, she had fled this place for the last time, disappearing a world away to Spain, where she had given up her name, Isadora Victorine Lugo, and the few possessions she had with her and become a postulant of the Benedictine sisters.

On her eighteenth birthday, she had taken her sacred vows and the name Sister Ria, leaving immediately for the order's convent in Poona. She had worked there in the mission hospital for seven years—a region of death from typhoid, cholera, and smallpox, but that had not frightened her, because God had been with her. Nor had her choice three years ago, when she and several other sisters volunteered to live and work inside a walled and guarded village of lepers in an uninhabited valley outside the ancient city.

She had made her decision for her Lord. Even so, the last three years had not been easy. She took a deep breath of the sea air and held it. The smell had been the worst of it. The fetid odor of the lepers' sores had nauseated her. She had prayed that the sense of disgust for the rotting flesh would leave her—that she could receive it as though it were Christ. But that had not happened. She squeezed her hands together until her knuckles turned white.

Still, she had been doing God's work, so it had been bearable. What seemed almost unbearable was her return to this place.

Exhausted, Sister Ria let out her breath, leaned back into the worn leather seat, and listened to the sounds of the horses laboring in their traces. She said a small prayer to Saint Francis to lessen their exertions, then smoothed the long black material of her wimple with an awkward movement of her hands, making certain her face was properly framed, her neck covered by the white cloth of her couvre-chef. Rivulets of sweat were running down her back and over her buttocks. She clamped her knees together and sat working on what she would say to him.

As she debated with herself, something moved on the seat in front of her. She jumped and saw an old yellow cat climb out from behind a pile of mailbags and sit down in the shadows. His ears were flattened, as if somebody had hit him over the head with a board, and he looked peeved at the world. She smiled. "How did you get in here, *viejo?*"

The cat didn't answer; he just meowed and seemed to be trying to appear dainty. But he was too big and rough-looking to be convincing, and he was hurt, an eye freshly gouged out and blood caked on his fur. She started to reach for him, but he spat and limped away across the seat. He looked badly beaten up. Sister Ria's face hardened into her best nursing countenance. "I have to examine you," she said in a firm voice. The cat hissed and backed farther away.

She eyed him carefully: He was very big and very ill-tempered-looking. She drew a deep breath and said in an even firmer voice, "Did you hear me?" In response, the old tom arched his back and let forth a horrible sound from somewhere deep inside him. She shrugged as if she heard that same terrifying sound every day and was bored by it. "Listen," she continued. The cat spat once more as if to emphasize the awful things he was going to do if she persisted, then he bared his sizable fangs at her.

"I'm not afraid of you," she lied.

Sister Ria raised a trembling hand and wiggled her fingers in the air like the legs of a tarantula. She watched the hand as if it belonged to someone else. The old cat watched it as well, teeth bared, ready to pounce. Then, with a hard snap of her wiggling fingers, Sister Ria grabbed him behind his neck with her other hand.

He never had a chance.

✝

It was late afternoon, and Sister Ria had lowered the canvas curtains against the dust and sunlight. She was holding the old feline—whom she had christened Fernando, after the Franciscan mission north of the pueblo—forcibly pinned down on her lap. He had just tried to bite her for the hundredth time, and she tightened her grip on the scruff of his neck. Having completed her examination of his injuries, she was convinced none were fatal. He in turn seemed convinced she was mentally defective. He looked at her with his one eye as if to say as much.

Suddenly, the stagecoach's wheels slipped into deep sand. She forgot her little war with Fernando and pulled up the window curtain.

The driver was reining the sweating horses through heavy stone pillars, slowing them to a prancing walk down a sandy drive bordered by ancient pepper trees. The drive turned and twisted to an enormous house set back under towering sycamores. The house had the look of a Renaissance villa, with heavy stone arches and colonnades, its white walls covered in beautiful flowering vines of wisteria and bougainvillea.

When the coach stopped, Sister Ria of the Benedictine Order of the Sisters of Mercy held the struggling Fernando out in front of her at a safe distance and stepped into the late-afternoon heat. She fought the trembling in her body.

She was home.

CHAPTER 3

THE HACIENDA WAS COOL and quiet, and Sister Ria stood looking at it as if the heavy stuccoed walls might suddenly rush her. She could hear the coach moving down the long drive and wished she were on it. Fernando lay momentarily still in her arms. She turned in a slow circle. Sister Ria had always known the house was beautiful; she had simply forgotten how beautiful.

The grand entry hall soared two stories above her, the thick walls plastered the color of a sun-ripened peach and textured in *rajueleado,* small embedded stones covering the surface in dramatic patterns. In the center of the entry was a low pool of water, a single spray rippling its still surface. The shadowy spaces looked arabesque. She stopped and stared into deeper shadows against a far wall. There was a man in a dark business suit and a small brimmed hat sitting on a hard-backed chair. He was watching her.

"May I help you, Sister?" he asked.

"No, I live here," she said. Then she quickly corrected herself. "I once lived here. This is my father's house."

The man nodded.

She smiled. "And now may I help you, sir?"

The man shook his head.

"Does anyone know you're here?"

"Yes, and I'm fine."

Sister Ria studied his face and then said, "I'll see that someone takes care of you."

"There's no need," he said.

Since it was not unusual for cattle and horse buyers to stop at the rancho, Sister Ria wasn't surprised by the man sitting on the chair. She moved deeper into the house, her eyes darting over the rooms. The walls were painted in earthy, pale colors from dusty cream to melon, the ceilings braced with rough-hewn beams. There were baroque touches, giant giltwood mirrors and huge silver candelabras, contrasting with the delicate grace of French officers' chairs and other furnishings, all distinctly different, all beautiful, all covered in fine fabrics of the same harmonious shades, all of it close to the patina of the old house. Her father, Don Maximiato Lugo, was a genius with the hue and look of things. But that was his only act of genius, she reflected.

Sister Ria was walking down the long central hallway of the house when she sensed someone watching her. She turned quickly around. The hallway was empty. "Hello?" she called. No answer. She shrugged her shoulders. "Just memories," Sister Ria said to Fernando. The old cat ignored her.

She turned and entered a sparsely furnished room and stopped, her eyes fixed on a portrait of a woman and a boy that hung suspended by two long gold chains. The woman's smile touched something deep inside her, and tears began to fill her eyes. "I came," she whispered. Seeing them again—her mother and older brother, Ramón—she wondered, as she always did: Why had the Lord taken them, leaving her with him?

She brushed the material of her habit as if trying to clear away her thoughts, knelt and prayed for their souls, then crossed herself and stood and reached up and touched the frame. As she was doing this, she heard a faint sound behind her. She turned around. The sound was coming from the west wall of the room. She walked over and stood listening. At first there was nothing. But slowly she began to sense some sort of movement behind the thick adobe. She knew that her grandfather had had narrow passageways constructed between the hacienda's load-bearing walls to allow workers to periodically check and repair the vulnerable mud bricks.

She put her ear to the plaster and listened again. Silence. But there had been something moving behind the wall. She was certain of it. Most likely it was one of the workers. Or it might be a ground squirrel that had dug its way in through an outside wall. That, she knew, could be a problem. Built of plastered-over mud and straw, the house depended greatly on its walls never being undermined by water or burrowing animals. She would let the head servant know.

Then she started walking again, fighting to maintain her grip on Fernando.

"This used to be my home," she said to the old cat. If he cared, Fernando did not show it. Sister Ria walked on.

She had been born in this hacienda in the year 1854. The rancho was thirty-seven thousand acres of a Spanish land grant inherited by her father from his father, and named La Cienega after the marshlands at the foot of the Sierra Santa Monicas. She had once believed it was a gift from God. She no longer had this feeling.

She stopped and listened.

The house was silent. The quiet reminded her of the mornings of her childhood when she would get up while the earth was still dark, and walk barefoot over the red tiles of the wide veranda, her feet numb from the cold floor, her head feeling light from the intense silence. She would stand looking at this world that belonged to her father, feeling that he might be a king of sorts. Yet she had learned that he was not a king. He was not even a good man. She winced at the thought and asked God to forgive her unkind acts of judgment.

Still, in her heart, she knew she was right.

Sister Ria heard footsteps and turned to see an old servant woman in a long black skirt and white blouse, walking briskly down the main hallway toward her, carrying an ebony cane in both hands like it was a spear. The woman looked thin and gray but not weak. She neither smiled nor seemed surprised to find a nun with a cat in her arms standing in the great hall of the hacienda. She stopped and leaned on her walking stick, looking as though she could put the stout tool to good purpose, and bowed slightly. "Sister?"

Sister Ria just stood. Then she forgot herself and, clutching the struggling Fernando tight against her, ran and threw an arm around the woman. "Oh, Aba, Aba," she cried. The servant began to pull away. "Aba, it's Isadora."

The woman clamped a tiny pair of spectacles onto the narrow bridge of her nose and peered into Sister Ria's face. "Child," she said, putting a hand to the back of Sister Ria's head and pulling her into her shoulder. "You are home."

"You look wonderful," Sister Ria said, bouncing on the balls of her feet. "I've missed you so."

The old servant's eyes moved slowly over Sister Ria's dark, shapeless habit and the stark white bands framing her face. From the look in her eyes, Sister Ria was certain the woman was recalling the long, unpleasant trip she had made fourteen years before to the convent at Guaymas to retrieve this stubborn child who stood before her now as a grown woman. "Does he know what you have become?"

"No."

"He will not be pleased."

"It is no longer his place."

"Isadora." The woman's voice was sharp.

Sister Ria held out the cat as if he were a peace offering. "His name is Fernando. He's hurt."

Aba did not take him. Instead, she continued to eye Sister Ria's dark habit and the large wooden cross hanging at her side.

"Aba."

Reluctantly, the servant tucked her walking stick under an arm and took hold of the old feline. Fernando stiffened as if he had been given a jolt of electricity, then he lashed out at Aba's thin hand before springing free and bounding off into the depths of the house. The woman took an expert cut at him with her long black cane. She missed, but just.

"I will have him destroyed," she said.

"Aba, don't tease."

The woman turned and started down the loggia. "Come with me, Isadora."

Sister Ria wiped the dampness from her eyes, clasped her hands in front of her waist, and followed in the slower walk of the convent, her eyes locked on the thin back of the old servant as if she were afraid the woman might disappear. "Aba—"

"Not now."

"But there's a man sitting in the entry."

The old woman continued walking.

The loggia was paved in worn slate that followed the contours of the earth, the walls lined with floor-to-ceiling bookshelves, wall sconces spilling muted light in yellow pools down its cavelike length. Aba stopped in front of a heavy wooden door that looked ancient in the shadowy light. Sister Ria stopped a few feet behind her.

"Go ahead, Isadora."

"He's not in jail?"

"Under arrest—but not in jail."

"Then the man—"

"—works for the sheriff."

"Did you know her?"

"Who?"

"Dorothy Regal?"

"Knock on the door, child."

Sister Ria pulled herself up straighter and stepped forward and knocked softly. There was no answer. She knocked again. No sound came from the room.

"You have more strength than that, Isadora."

She knocked harder. Still no response. She pushed down on the heavy brass handle and slowly opened the door. Then she heard the sharp tap of Aba's cane against the floor and turned back. The old woman stepped forward, placed her hands on Sister Ria's shoulders, and slowly turned her around until she was facing the open doorway again. "You will show proper respect," she said, straightening the coarse black material of Sister Ria's wimple.

"He is not the pope, Aba."

"You will show respect, child." It was not a request. Then she adjusted the heavy material of the habit on Sister Ria's thin shoulders. "Your robes are filthy."

"I have been traveling."

Aba brushed dust from the cloth. "Regardless, you will show respect," she repeated, smoothing a wrinkle with her thin hand. She grasped Sister Ria's shoulders again and squeezed gently. Sister Ria nodded and stepped inside.

The room was every bit as strange in appearance as she remembered. The windows were shuttered, and the long red drapes that spilled over the floor had been pulled shut, making the room as dark as the hallway. There was a candelabra burning in the center, tossing soft dancing light over everything. Her father had always loved the Muslim worlds of Afghanistan, Morocco, and Persia, had traveled those lands in his youth; his bedroom was filled with the trappings of those places, exotic silk fabrics and scimitars, hookahs, damask-covered cushions, Oriental taborets, an exotic mixture of his personal fetishes. There was the smell of leather and scented oils, and wisps of incense hung in the air.

Even odder was the fact that the room was cluttered with baskets of fruit and candies and eggs. There were also bunches of flowers—some fresh, some dead—lying on the floor and hanging from the ceiling. Hand-built willow crates stacked around the room contained dozens of live rabbits, chickens, and ducks, the smell of their droppings mixing with the sharp odor of incense. While offensive, the smell was nowhere near as suffocating as the stench of the dying lepers.

Sister Ria stood near the door and let her eyes adjust to the weak light of the room. "Respect," Aba said from the hallway. Sister Ria looked back at the old woman and curtsied like a child. Then she felt bad and said, "Yes."

She turned back to the room and stared at a small gold-painted table that supported the symbols of his odd collective sense of God: a crucified Christ, a sixteenth-century portrait of Buddha, a framed verse from the Koran. The sacristy of his life. Studying the Christ, Sister Ria tensed and crossed herself and continued to look around the room. The bed was empty. He was nowhere to be seen. A large armoire stood open against one wall, and she glimpsed his beautiful garments—bright tunics, afghans, jubbahs, kimonos—dozens of them. Then she saw him.

He was lying on a stone platform in a corner of the room, dressed in a medieval Japanese suit of armor made of small lacquered pieces of bamboo laced together to form an apronlike skirt, and another set of bamboo plates that draped like a stiff shawl over his back and shoulders.

"What are you doing, Father?"

"Contemplating my death." His voice was weak, and he looked thin, with deep sunken eyes underscored by black circles.

"I see," she said, a sense of the old resistance creeping into her words, giving them an edge and surprising her after all these years, after all her prayers. She fought the feeling and said in a calm voice, "It is Sister Ria." She caught herself and said, "It's Isadora. I have—"

"Contemplate your death."

"I am not here to contemplate."

Suddenly, a hen in one of the cages began to cackle, and the egg she had just laid slipped through the bottom slats and smashed onto the floor below. Sister Ria was looking for something to clean it up with when Don Maximiato Lugo began to stir. Slowly, as if it were a tremendous effort, he brought his thin legs over the edge of the coffinlike structure and pushed himself into a seated position. He struggled to put on a metal samurai skull piece with heavy leather flaps that protected his neck. She watched him. He looked unsteady, his head moving over his thin shoulders under the weight of the helmet, his deep-set eyes red, tearing, and unfocused.

"It has been a long time, Father."

He did not respond.

"You do not look well," she said finally.

He peered at her with his head tilted at an odd angle.

She realized at that moment that he wasn't here, that he was lost in one of his drugged and senseless stupors. As if in response to her thoughts, a young Chinese boy entered the room carrying a tray with an opium pipe on it. He stopped when he saw her. She shook her head and pointed toward the door. "Please leave," she told the boy. "There will be no more of that in this house," she continued, sounding every bit the convent nurse even to herself.

"I will decide what will and will not take place in this house," Don Maximiato snapped.

"Please leave," Sister Ria said again to the boy. All the long years of caring for the sick and dying caused her to stiffen at the smell and sight of the filth in the room. She looked at the young servant and said, "Have these animals removed and this room cleaned."

Uncertain what to do, the boy set down the tray and bowed toward Sister Ria. Then he bowed again, this time toward the old man, and began to scurry for the door. "Young man," she said. The boy froze.

"Have you come to order me around?" Don Maximiato asked.

"No."

The boy was turning from Sister Ria to her father.

"You have no right—"

"You are correct, I have no right." She paused. "May we give the animals to the workers?"

"No. They are sacred offerings."

Sister Ria studied her father's face before turning slowly to the boy. "Give them to the poor. To anyone in need."

The boy bowed quickly and left.

24

The old man seemed to drift off again. His eyes had lost their focus, and he looked as though he might fall over. "I will pray for you. Whatever your affliction," he mumbled, clasping his hands together.

"Do not pray for me, Father. Please—do not." She stopped abruptly as if the words hurt.

Don Maximiato raised his head and looked at her, his eyes narrowing, his face flushing. All at once he seemed alert and aware of his surroundings. "You will not tell me what I can and cannot do in my own house!" he shouted. He spun and picked up the tray with the opium pipe and flung these, smashing glass over the floor.

Sister Ria walked to the bed and leaned against a tall canopy post, looking at the back of her father's helmeted head. Memories beginning to stir. "After eleven years," she whispered. Her hands were shaking, and she grasped the wooden post, squeezing it with her fingers. "You haven't changed. You never will." Her voice was rising.

Sister Ria had turned to leave when she saw it. It was an enormous life-size painting of her older brother, Ramón, hanging on the far wall of the room. She walked slowly toward it, her eyes pooling with moisture. The painting looked so lifelike that Sister Ria moaned, "Oh, Ramón—"

Don Maximiato bolted upright on the stone platform. "I have told you never to say that name in this house again!"

Sister Ria whirled angrily and faced her father.

"Isadora," Aba said through the open doorway.

Sister Ria hesitated and then composed herself and turned and started toward the door. Behind her, Don Maximiato said, "I did not ask you to come here."

She turned back and stared at him. His eyes were closed again. She cleared her throat and quietly said, "No, you did not." She studied his face for what seemed a long time before she said, "I came because I promised Mother I would come." She paused. "I came to ask you if you murdered that woman."

He opened his eyes and looked up at her, scratching his chin as if perplexed.

"Please—don't mock me. I do not deserve that," she said.

He dismissed her with a wave of his hand.

Sister Ria continued to watch him. "I'll wait for your answer," she said, then left the room.

✝

Evening had brought a cold breeze laden with moisture from the sea. Sister Ria stood in the shadows of the loggia, looking out a window at the distant fields shading purple in the fading light. She was remembering things she didn't want to remember. She smiled weakly to herself. "He is the same."

Aba was standing behind her. "He is your father," she said.

"The things in his room—"

"Yes?"

"Why?"

"Some believe—" Aba said, crossing her arms over her breasts.

"Believe what?"

"That the patrón is sainted."

Sister Ria raised her eyebrows. "Mad, perhaps."

"He is the patrón. He is your father. You will not speak of him in that manner."

"My father? In all my years with him, he never once called me daughter. Not once, Aba."

The old woman looked steadily at the back of Sister Ria's veil. "It is not important. He is the patrón," she said firmly.

Sister Ria shook her head. "It is important. To me."

They stood for a while without speaking, the old woman watching the young nun, Sister Ria gazing blindly out the window at the dark land. Finally, Sister Ria said, "My sister, Milagros?"

"She was written to. She has not come." There was a cold sound to the words.

"You never cared for Milagros."

The old woman waited a moment before she said, "Were you taught rudeness at this convent, or is it just your nature?"

"She will come," Sister Ria said softly. "In the meantime, there are things we must do. The Chinese boy?"

"Min."

As soon as Aba had spoken his name, the young man stepped out of a nearby doorway where he had been waiting silently. Sister Ria jumped at the sight of him. Min grinned and then bowed, remaining bent over.

"Stand up, please. You should not bow to me," Sister Ria said. Aba shot her a stern look, but Sister Ria ignored her.

The boy straightened, the grin cutting his face in half, and slipped his hands into the long sleeves of his gown of yellow Chinese silk. He had tied a matching ribbon smartly in his pigtail.

"I have told Min to remove the animals and to have Father's room cleaned."

"The patrón will not allow it," Aba said.

Sister Ria ignored the comment. "Do we have carbolic acid?" she asked, sounding once more like the convent nurse. "If we do, have the servants use it on the floors. And the curtains in the patrón's room must be taken down so sunlight can be let in." She hesitated, then went on, "And no more animals or opium are to be taken to his room."

"He will allow none of this."

"He is not well, and these things must be done." Sister Ria spoke in the tone she had often used to urge reluctant laborers to accomplish tasks at the poor convent hospital.

"We are not the patrón."

"For the patrón's own good."

Aba thought about this. "Perhaps I will attempt these things, Isadora," she said, "but only if you show him proper respect."

Sister Ria smiled at the old woman. Aba had always stood between her and her father, balancing the imbalance of their two lives. Sister Ria loved her for many things, but she loved her especially for that. "Yes," she said, "the respect he deserves."

Aba caught the tone. "Isadora, do not play games with me. You are no longer a child."

Sister Ria clasped her hands at the waist and nodded. She cleared her throat and said, "Thank you for sending the cable."

The old woman was checking the time on a large pendulum clock against the time on her own small pocket watch. She looked at Sister Ria. "I'm sorry. I did not hear you."

"The cable. Thank you for sending it."

Aba adjusted the minute hand on the large clock. "I sent no cable." In a scolding tone, she said, "I did not know where you were."

"Then who sent it?"

The woman shrugged and tightened the shawl around her shoulders.

They had been standing in the hallway for close to an hour, Aba waiting patiently, as she had on Sister Ria's mother, then, after her mother's death, on Milagros. Sister Ria looked out the window at the last of evening, wondering again about the cable. She gave up.

"I'm tired, Aba."

The woman tipped her head and began walking down the loggia with her brisk stride, her cane held at the ready. Sister Ria quickly fell behind, and though she tried to resist, she glanced around her. The convent rule of modesty of the eyes seemed pointless in this house.

She stopped in front of a large oil painting in a magnificent gold frame. Candles in wall sconces burned on either side, casting soft light over the lovely scene. Her father had painted it the year she left—an old woman watching a passing throng of sheep and goats, herd dogs and sun-weathered shepherds moving down a summer road. The old woman in the scene was not Aba; he had never painted Aba. Aba had been the head servant at La Cienega for over forty years—Don Maximiato painting for hours every day, using maids and field hands by the dozens as models in his work—but he had never painted Aba.

Sister Ria swallowed hard and looked down at the floor. Except for one time—a time she still did not understand—he had never painted her, either. She squeezed her hands together until they hurt. She hadn't come back to pity herself. She had come because of her mother. Nothing more, nothing less.

Her eyes returned to the painting. She could almost hear the sounds and see the movement in the still liquid of the canvas. In his youth, her father had studied in Paris and Rome. He was an accomplished artist, there was no refuting that. But that was the only testament she could make on his behalf.

Aba had stopped walking and stood looking back at her, frowning. The old woman tapped her stick twice on the floor, the noise echoing against the walls. Sister Ria jumped at the sound and pulled her clasped hands tighter into her waist and looked down at the floor. "I'm sorry, Aba," she said, knowing the old woman hated idleness.

Aba watched her a moment longer and then shook her head and asked, "Have you forgotten all that I taught?"

"No."

"Then when you talk to me, look at me. And speak up. You are the daughter of the patrón."

Sister Ria raised her head. "Everything is fine, Aba."

"No, it is not. But it will become so. You will learn respect for your father, and you will learn to behave properly. At all times." Aba turned and continued down the hall.

Sister Ria did not sleep in her bedroom that night. Instead, she took a heavy blue blanket and returned to the hallway in front of her father's room, pulled a large leather wing chair directly opposite his door, and sat. She pulled the crumpled yellow cable from her pocket and read it again. There was a curious phrase at the bottom that she sensed she had seen before but could not place: *May you pardon my intrusion.* She shrugged and put away the paper. It mattered little who had cabled her. She was certain the person's intentions had been good.

She dozed off and on throughout the night into the early-morning hours, as if keeping a death vigil, fully awakening only when Aba brought her a tray of coffee and small sweet cakes. The old woman remained standing nearby, watching her hold the cup in both hands and sip the liquid through a cloud of steam. Sister Ria ignored the servant and peered through the rising vapors of her coffee at the heavy door to Don Maximiato's room, as if determined to will the old man to come out and face her.

"This is not right, child. Go to your bedroom before the other servants see you. It is unseemly."

Sister Ria shook her head.

"He will not do as you wish."

"Then he will have no peace."

31

It was the old woman's turn to shake her head. Then she stopped, remembering her position, bowed stiffly, and said, "Is there anything you need?"

"No, thank you."

Aba nodded and walked down the long hallway.

"I love you," Sister Ria called after her.

If she heard, Aba did not respond.

"Aba," she called louder. The old woman stopped but did not turn around. "I heard a noise yesterday afternoon behind the west wall in the gallery room. I presume the workers are repairing the bricks."

"There are no repairs being made to the walls."

"Then an animal has gotten into the passageway."

"I will have someone check," Aba said. The old woman started down the hallway again.

The head servant obviously had told the other servants to stay out of the main hallway, since the time on the nearby pendulum clock read 12:10 in the afternoon, and none of the house workers had appeared. Then Sister Ria heard the heavy metal lock on the bedroom door turn. A small crack appeared, and through it she glimpsed a narrow strip of her father's face peering out at her. She sat up straighter. Hurriedly, Don Maximiato closed the door and locked it again. Sister Ria said nothing.

When Aba came down the hallway an hour later, she was followed by the Chinese boy, Min, who carried a heavy tray of food and drink. Aba bowed her head politely at Sister Ria and unlocked the door to the patrón's bedroom, letting Min enter. Then the old servant turned and stood outside the door, her arms crossed over her thin chest, ignoring Sister Ria.

"I will not force my way into the room," Sister Ria said.

Aba ignored the comment. Moments later, she said, "I had the gallery wall checked. There was no animal."

"I heard something."

"There was no animal."

"Thank you for checking," Sister Ria said.

Min came out of the room minutes later, carrying a pottery waste jar. He bowed at Sister Ria, and he and Aba marched down the hallway, leaving Sister Ria to her silent watch. Twice that afternoon, Min delivered food and drink to her. On his second trip, the boy stood looking at her sympathetically, but he was too well trained to speak to the patrón's daughter of personal matters.

"I am fine," she said, as if reading his mind.

He smiled and started to bow.

"No, please—"

He stood and grinned and walked off down the hall.

Periodically throughout the afternoon, Aba would step out into the hallway from a distance and check to see that Sister Ria was still there. Each time the old servant would shake her head and then retreat. Tiring of the chair, Sister Ria began to pace back and forth in front of the door; twice she made a quick trip to the new water closet that had been installed down the hallway. The house was silent, and she felt alone—sensations she had lived with for the past eleven years. She would outlast him, she told herself.

———

He could not stay locked in his room much longer. He simply did not have the patience for it. He hated restraint of any kind. His life, she knew, was an odd whipsawing of irrational whims and impulses. No, he could not last inside his bedroom for very long. And when he came out, she would ask him again if he had murdered the woman. If he said yes, there would be nothing she could do for him beyond prayer. Her breath caught in her throat—but if he said no? She trembled, realizing she had no idea what she would do if his answer was no. Just as abruptly, the trembling stopped, and she felt calmer. She was certain of his guilt. She went back to staring at his bedroom door.

Don Maximiato restrained himself throughout the evening. To her surprise, he failed to appear that night and through the next day. To her greater surprise, her own patience was badly stretched. She began to pace in front of his door in a very un-Christian way.

"You have behaved like this all of your life," she said through the thick wooden door. "It worked when I was a child. But I am no longer a child, and it will no longer work. Do you hear?"

She put an ear to the door and listened. No sound.

"I know you are in there."

Nothing.

"I am not going away."

Silence.

She brought her hands, palms together, to her face. "And you will not anger me. Do you hear that as well?"

If he did, he did not reply.

The hours began to pass more slowly. She continued to pace,

reciting the rosary, the Nicene Creed, the Lord's Prayer, the Twenty-third Psalm. Not until the middle of the following day did he emerge. She was certain he had a spy hole somewhere in the wall or door of his room, since he caught her completely by surprise as she sat in the water closet. She heard the great door opening on its heavy iron hinges and small footsteps sneaking quickly down the hallway.

"You wait right there," she said through a narrow crack in the bathroom door.

He did not wait.

"I want to talk to you," she called, rushing to get her habit on straight.

She caught up with Don Maximiato as he headed through the library's large French doors that opened onto the hacienda's rose garden. He was dressed in a beautiful green caftan and moving fast. She pressed her lips together and marched after him down a narrow brick pathway edged on both sides by deep green foliage, then through a large red gate set in a great brown mud wall. She pulled the gate shut behind her so that he could not escape, and she turned around. It was as if she had been transported to Morocco. The enclosure behind the gate was covered with a floor of sand, while a tent of black camel hair stood in the center, surrounded by palms and olive trees. The only thing missing, she thought, was a small herd of goats. She shook her head at his playacting.

"Father, we need to talk."

The patrón paid no attention to her. He sat on a small stool and took off his sandals and then washed his face at a stone fountain and his feet in a tiled tank sunk in the sand. Not once did he look in her direction, as if oblivious to the fact that she was standing only a few feet away. He spread a small blue and red carpet on the sand in front of the tent and knelt and closed his eyes in meditation. She was directly in front of him, standing with her hands on her hips.

"Father," she said, "stop what you are doing and listen. I need to—" She hesitated. He was obviously at his midday prayers. The shame of interrupting a man at prayer caused her to step back and stop talking.

He opened one eye and looked at her. "You should be veiled," he said.

"I'm not a Muslim."

"You should be veiled," he repeated.

"I'm not a Muslim," she said again, slowly, for emphasis.

"You should be veil—"

"Enough! Please."

There was the hint of a satisfied smile on his face. His lips were pressed together so that he looked like a lizard that had just swallowed a fly. He shut his eye.

She studied him closely: the remains of a decent-looking face, a high, thin nose, hair gone thin and white, cheeks sunken. He looked tired, his body far thinner than she had remembered. He was speaking Arabic now. She waited out of respect for God, not him.

When he had finished, Don Maximiato stood and shook the small rug and began to roll it into a neat tube. Sister Ria inched closer. She opened her mouth and then quickly shut it. She had rehearsed this moment every day for the past two months, how she would do this and say that, but now that it was here, all she could do was open and shut her mouth like a wooden puppet.

He stopped rolling the carpet and looked up and said, "May I help you?"

She clasped her hands at her waist and nodded.

He grew impatient. "If you have something to say, please say it."

"I have tried to forgive you," she blurted, "but I cannot."

He shrugged. "I don't need it."

"I need it," she snapped.

"Adding up your little hurts?"

"They are not little hurts!"

"I thought you had come to ask if I was a murderer," Don Maximiato said, dancing a playful jig in the sand and then turning and walking out the gate and back up the narrow garden path to the house. Sister Ria trailed behind him, her face red with rage.

"It has taken me years to be able to do this," she said as they moved down the long hallway. "You cannot just walk off as if nothing happened. Do you understand?"

Don Maximiato yawned and kept walking.

When they were halfway down the hall, Don Maximiato broke into a sprint. Sister Ria bolted after him. The old man feinted left into a nearby corridor, and Sister Ria took the fake and turned off. Immediately, she whirled around and rushed back into the loggia and saw Don Maximiato walking calmly into his bedroom.

She stomped in after him. "You will not walk off!"

"Isadora."

Sister Ria stood opening and clenching her hands, glaring at her father as he crawled up onto his bed. Then she turned and faced Aba.

"Come here, child," the old servant said.

The old man fluffed his pillows, then picked up his sketch pad and pencil, leaned back, and began to draw.

Sister Ria turned back to him and collected herself before she said, "I loved you, and you sliced my heart out." She studied his face for a long time. "But you are right. I have come because I promised Mother I would come. And so I ask you again, did you kill that woman?"

He said nothing.

"Isadora," the old woman repeated, "come out of the room."

"I will wait for your answer. I swear."

He stuck his tongue out at her.

In response, she tipped a basket of peaches sitting on the table onto the floor. The fruit rolled in every direction. She walked out.

Sister Ria once again refused to leave the hallway in front of her father's bedroom, taking up her position in the large leather chair while Aba stood and watched her. They said nothing to each other. Sister Ria was shamefully aware that she had sunk to his childish level in her attempt to force him to tell her the truth. But surely God understood.

Sister Ria was not certain when she had fallen asleep or when she had been taken to her room. The exhaustion of two months of difficult traveling, little food, and less sleep had taken its full toll at last. She sat up in bed and looked around her. Her room had not changed. It was as if she had just stepped out into the hallway for a moment and returned. Her childhood clothes still hung in the French armoire, her mirror and brushes still lay on her dressing table. Aba had dressed her in her nightgown and opened the door to the central garden.

Sister Ria breathed in deeply the smell of roses, her eyes moving over the things of her past, slowly transported by memory back some seventeen years to the time when her only name was Isadora. She had not thought him mad before. Obsessive and given to strange fixations, yes, but not mad. The actual insanity—the cold hard core of it—had come full-fleshed with their deaths. She closed her eyes and thought of that day when she had first seen it masking his face.

It was a warm summer morning one week after the deaths of her mother and brother from smallpox. She was eleven years old and standing in this same room with its thick adobe walls and the window stuffed with pillows where she often played dolls or daydreamed. The window opened onto the courtyard garden of bougainvillea, orange and lemon trees, and roses. Roses were everywhere. They were her father's favorite. The beds overflowed with them, with their magnificent range of color—yellow, orange, peach, red—and delicious fragrance.

On this morning, she was surrounded by three or four of the Indian and Mexican women who worked in the house. They were quietly caring for her. The room was damp with the warm smell of perfume and bathwater. Aba, who had been the hacienda's head servant since be-

fore Isadora's birth, was combing her long dark hair while the others dressed her in a white dress of satin that her mother had bought for her the year before. Then suddenly her father was there, yelling and cursing and driving the women out of the room. Only Aba remained, standing loyally, defiantly, in front of her.

"You will no longer dress her like a girl," he said. "You may dress her sister in that manner, but not this child."

Her father was not a large man—he was thin and shorter than Aba—but in his rage, he seemed a giant to Isadora. He held clothing in his hand.

"She is a girl, Don Maximiato," Aba said. "Soon to be a young lady. She needs to begin to dress like one." Her voice was firm.

"Do not lecture me, woman. You will not pamper this child. She will not wear dresses."

"There is a mass this afternoon for Ramón, Father," Isadora said.

"There is no mass, and you will not speak of Ramón again. Put on these pants and this shirt," he said, tossing the clothes onto the bed. Isadora recognized the shirt as one that Ramón had outgrown years before.

Aba was still standing between them. Trembling, Isadora took a step to the side. It was the first time in her life she had tried to defy him. "There is a mass. And I will go."

"No, you will not." There was a blue vein pulsing dangerously at the side of his head, and a look on his face of intense concentration—the way Millie had looked that day on the beach. He turned and faced the servant. "And you will shave her head."

"It is not right," Aba said.

"I did not ask you, woman."

Aba did not move.

"You will do these things!" he shouted.

Sister Ria refused to cry. She lay back on her pillows and tried to forget. From the angle of the moonlight in the open doorway, she knew that it was well past midnight. Moist air drifting in from the garden carried the smell of plant growth, and she could see the ancient stone pergola and, behind it, the terraced walls. But her thoughts were not on the moonlight or the garden. They were focused instead on the familiar sense of bitterness that had risen in her.

"Forgive me, Lord. I've tried—" For the past eleven years, she had hidden her hatred beneath the daily cycle of convent prayers and the never-ending hours spent nursing the sick and dying. But two months ago, when she received the cable, it had begun to stir in her again.

She pounded her hand on the pillow. "I don't know how to stop!"

She fought the trembling in her body and looked around in growing desperation. The house was silent. Her gaze moved slowly over the room, stopping at the closed door that led to the side room where they had found Elsie. "I miss you," she whispered. Slowly, she calmed herself and listened to the night wind. She was lying back on her pillows when the old cat jumped silently up onto the end of the bed and sat arrogantly with his back to her.

Thankful for the distraction, she wiped the dampness from her face on the sheets and smiled. "There you are. Shame on you for scratching poor Aba. Until you learn to behave, I'm calling you Fern." She narrowed her eyes at the old tom. "Do you hear me?"

Fernando looked at her with an expression that said he was more annoyed that she was talking to him than by whatever she chose to call him. She could see that his eye socket had been flushed and salved and the dried dirt and blood washed from his fur. Around his neck was tied a poultice of some sort. Sister Ria felt a surge of love for the old servant.

Fernando was turning back to the shadows when Sister Ria heard something scrape on the tile floor and knew that someone or something besides the cat was in the darkness with her. She opened her mouth slightly so that her breathing would not interfere with her hearing, and listened for another sound, her eyes probing the layers of night surrounding the bed. Nothing. Then she saw a dark humanlike shape in a corner of the room.

"Aba?"

Silence.

"Is that you?"

There was no response.

"Father?"

The only answer was a sharp metallic sound, a hard snap of metal that seemed to trigger an explosion of noise and movement in the darkness. Something alive and maniacal was rushing back and forth in the shadows, banging into furniture.

Then the room fell silent, and she probed the shadows with her eyes. The figure was gone. She was taking small bites of air and shaking hard. A familiar odor was drifting in the air. She waited. Moments later, she heard footsteps outside in the garden, then the closing of a door.

She continued to wait.

Nothing moved. When she could no longer bear the waiting, she lit the candle on the nightstand, the light tossing distorted shadows against the walls. Her breath caught in her throat. Slowly, she crossed the floor and held the candle closer to the wall, then backed away. Someone had smeared a rough Latin cross in blood on the plaster. She could not take her eyes off it, as if God Himself had made the mark against her.

There was movement on the floor again, and she jumped back and quickly raised the candle, casting a larger circle of light over the room. Blood was everywhere. The small head of a rooster was lying in a corner, the eyes gazing dull into the shadows. The lifeless body lay in another corner, the dead bird's wings still rising and falling slowly. Fernando was sitting close by it, watching the poor headless creature's last movements intently. Then one of the bird's legs stretched out, the claws closing as if trying to grasp the old cat. Fernando hopped away. The body was still now.

Sister Ria crossed herself, then, clutching her crucifix, unlocked her bedroom door and walked out into the long darkened hallway, stopping and listening, her eyes probing the gloom for the intruder. Nothing. There was a black emptiness between the massive adobe walls of the wide hallway. The only sound was the soft ticking of a clock. She saw that it was two A.M. Sister Ria crept forward and the old cat did the same, moving like a small leopard on the prowl, making a strange gnashing sound with his teeth.

Twenty minutes later, she had searched the library, the huge kitchen, the receiving room, the closets and storage pantries and other likely hiding places, and had found no one. The policeman was asleep in a chair on the veranda. Then the realization struck her: There was no intruder. It had been her father. He had killed the rooster and smeared the vile cross on the wall to frighten her.

Sister Ria trotted down the hall to her father's room and pounded on the locked door until her hands hurt. But he neither answered the door nor spoke. She stopped pounding and stood rubbing her hands together, leaning in close and listening. There was no sound. But she was certain he was inside, mocking her.

"You ruined my life," she shouted. "But you will not frighten me! Do you understand?"

She had turned and was starting back down the hallway to her bedroom when a shadow moved. She whirled and faced it and watched as Aba stepped into a shaft of pale moonlight that spilled into the loggia. The glow gave the old woman an ethereal look.

"Child?" Aba said to her. "What is the trouble?"

"Father was in my room," she said, rushing her words. She tried to calm herself, continuing more slowly, "He killed a *gallo* . . . then fled into the garden, then back into the house."

Aba was still dressed. She was drying her hands on a small towel.

"Father killed a rooster—"

"No, he did not. He was not in your room. He did not kill a rooster."

"Aba, there is blood everywhere. He killed a rooster—"

"There are thieves."

"It wasn't a thief." Sister Ria paused, trying to make sense of what had just happened. "Why would a thief kill something in my room?"

"Perhaps to frighten you away."

"It wasn't a thief."

"*Los ladrones,*" Aba said as if she hadn't heard, "believe that since the patrón is to be executed, he has hidden his gold in the walls of the hacienda."

The woman had begun walking down the darkened hallway toward Sister Ria's room. Sister Ria stared at the back of her head, waiting until she found her voice again. "What did you say?"

"That the thieves—"

"No—that he is to be executed."

The old servant turned and stood looking at her.

"Aba?"

"In eight days."

EIGHT DAYS

CHAPTER 4

THE NIGHT had seemed endless. Sister Ria was pacing back and forth in front of the patrón's bedroom, barely conscious of the *vit-vit-vit* sound of the swallows building their mud nesting cups under the eaves of the hacienda.

She had been sick twice during the night.

Aba leaned against a wall of the loggia and watched her. The old woman was framed in a patch of bright sunlight and looked as if she were finally in one of the patrón's paintings. "He does not deserve this, Isadora," she snapped.

"I am doing nothing to him."

"You are stalking back and forth in front of his room."

"I'm waiting, that's all."

"He doesn't deserve it."

Sister Ria looked at the woman, overcome by emotions that swirled in her like a kaleidoscope. "And what does he deserve, Aba?"

Aba pushed away from the wall, too quickly for the movement

to be perceived as anything but angry, and started to answer, then stopped.

"No," Sister Ria said, "forget that you are the head servant. Say whatever you wish. You believe he deserves better, Aba. Tell me what he deserves. Because I don't know."

Aba shook her head.

"Tell me."

When Aba spoke, the sound was almost inaudible. "Peace" was all she said. She began to retreat slowly down the hallway. She looked broken.

"Aba."

The servant stopped and raised her chin with her back to Sister Ria.

Sister Ria cleared her throat and said, "He deserves peace."

Aba nodded and continued down the hall.

Sister Ria watched until the woman had disappeared around a turn, and then she wrapped her arms around her shoulders, hugging herself. She stood trying to answer the nagging questions that surged like seawater through her brain. She had no answers. All she had was her promise to her mother and the fact that her father was going to die and she could not stop hating him.

It was a dark-staining sin.

Sister Ria sat down hard on the loggia floor and leaned back, exhausted, against the wall, her thoughts on a morning fifteen years earlier. She had been awakened by the night maid and told that her father was waiting for her in the hacienda's kitchen. She had dressed quickly, grabbing her boots and running barefoot down the loggia, fearing that something had happened to Millie.

He was smoking at the long table when she rushed into the room. "What's wrong, Father?"

"I want you out in the barn" was all he said.

"Why?"

He walked out without answering.

There were horses tied behind a wagon near the stables and riders sitting around a small fire. The men watched her, their stares betraying the fact that they had never seen a female of age in pants. She ignored them and looked at the horses. Most were old, some injured. And she knew their fate: The animals would be slaughtered for hides and tallow.

She shivered and raised the collar of her coat against the chill. They were approaching the huge stone stable. Lanterns burned inside.

"Why am I here, Father?"

"Bring your horse out and tie it with the others."

Isadora took a step back, as if she'd been physically struck. "No," she said. "Garrapata is a pet." The pony had been given to her by her godfather, José Vargas, on her fourth birthday. He was small and black, and she had named him Garrapata, the tick. She had ridden him every day as a child and babied him ever since.

Don Maximiato turned and faced her. "Place him with the others."

She shook her head. "He has nothing to do with these horses."

The patrón took a draw on his cigarette and broke into a hacking cough. When he stopped, he said, "You need a working animal."

"I'm not one of your horsemen."

Don Maximiato ignored her and started through the darkness toward the barn again, Isadora hurrying after him.

"I don't need a new horse. I don't want one!" she screamed. Then she stopped and struggled for control over her emotions. When she spoke again, she made her voice lower and more reasoned-sounding. She knew from long and painful experience that defying him would not work. "I'm sorry, Father. If you want Gar's stall, please take it. This is your stable—you should, of course, do as you wish. I'll put him in the pasture."

The old barn master, Auel, was waiting by the door. He tipped his head respectfully at the patrón. Don Maximiato stared down the long stone passageway between the stalls. It was empty. "Did I not tell you to have the animal out?"

The old man did not lift his head. "The pony is no trouble, Señor Lugo. And we have other empty stalls."

"Did I ask you these things?"

"No, Señor Lugo."

"No, I simply asked you to have the animal out of the stall."

"Yes, Señor Lugo," the old man said, hurrying away down the aisle.

Isadora ran after him, pulling on his arm. "Auel, you cannot do this. Gar is my horse! Isadora's horse, Auel. You cannot!"

The old Mexican stopped and looked into her face, his features lined with emotion. "I am old, child. I know no other work. I must do this."

Isadora held on to him for a few moments. Then she took a deep breath, the air jerking in her windpipe, let his arm go, and nodded. But she was not done. As soon as Auel entered the pony's stall, she padlocked it behind him and turned and stood glaring at her father.

"The key," he said, holding out his hand.

"No."

"Milagros said you would not have the strength to do this."

Isadora squinted hard and shook her head. "You are lying. Milagros didn't know anything about this. She would have told me."

He shrugged. "I have given you the chance to do it right."

"The chance to do it right!" she screamed. "To have Gar slaughtered? He is a pet. My pet! I am your daughter!"

"He is useless."

"He is a pet!"

The riders were watching them from the stable's huge open door. Don Maximiato glared at them, and they walked away. He turned back to her. "Unlock the stall and promise to keep the pony in the pasture, and I'll let you have him." He took a draw on his cigarette.

Isadora shook her head. "I don't believe you."

"Auel, take him out to the corral and get the stall ready for the new horse." Don Maximiato looked at Isadora. She didn't move. "Isn't that what you wanted?"

Isadora hesitated and then turned and unlocked the door. Her father nodded at the old man. "Remove him to the corral."

The old man trotted Garrapata out of the stall and down the long walkway toward the rear door of the stables. Isadora hurried beside the little horse. She was holding the pony's head when her father joined them. He put his hand on the animal's rump, ruffling his grizzled coat. "I am far too indulgent."

"No. You are being kind. And I thank you. I promise to keep him out of the barn. I promise." Isadora wiped her eyes on the back of her sleeve, then pulled the halter off the pony and hung it on the fence. She took a curry brush from a wooden box at the side of the corral and began to stroke Garrapata's coat.

Don Maximiato walked to the pony's head and scratched its ears. Her father was saying something that she couldn't hear, and she was combing the pony's long tail and smiling through tears at him, when his hand seemed to explode and Garrapata's head jerked back. The animal shuddered, then his legs buckled and he collapsed straight down.

Isadora shoved her father away. "Why?" she screamed, kneeling and cradling the dead pony's heavy head in her lap. "Why? Tell me why!"

Her father said nothing. He just slipped the small pistol into the pocket of his coat and started back toward the barn. Auel was leading a large, ugly roan into Garrapata's stall. Isadora stood and picked up a rock and threw it at her father. It missed, but just barely. "I hate you!" she yelled.

Never again did she trust him.

His unsound mind had made a convulsive assault on his behavior. He would fly into hysterical rages for no reason—throwing things, threatening her or the servants—only to retreat for days into isolated silence in his room, refusing food and drink, as if self-denial were penitence enough for his mad acts. Then, puzzlingly, he would emerge from his room, returned to a level of normalcy that was sufferable.

Now she sat and listened to the tiny swallows in the eaves of the house, rocking slowly back and forth, her thoughts returning to that dark morning in the corral.

"Why?" she had screamed again and again, her voice at last breaking off into sobs.

He stopped at the door to the stable. "Because you need a work horse. Because you need to keep up with the riders. Because you need to learn, if you are able—which I doubt—to run La Cienega." He was breathing hard. "Are those reasons enough for you?"

The anger continued to surge in her throat. "I am not one of your men. And I won't become one. I wear these clothes—that's enough! Do you hear? Enough!"

Isadora was glaring at her father when she saw her sister. Milagros was standing at the corner of the stable, watching, a white filigreed scarf over her head. When their eyes met, Millie broke into a run and knelt beside Isadora and held her in her arms. They cried together.

"He said you knew that he was going to do this." Isadora looked into Millie's face. "You didn't know, did you?"

"Of course not," Millie said, pulling her sister tight against her. "That's his lunacy talking."

Sister Ria was kneeling in the hallway in front of her father's room, praying for both their souls, when the door opened and the patrón walked out dressed as an English gentleman: black frock coat, towering top hat, and cane. In another time and place, she might have laughed. But not now. This time was horribly different. He was going to die. And Aba was right: He deserved respect. Respect given the condemned.

"Good morning, Father," she said quietly, then stood and stepped to the side to let him pass. "Is there anything I can do for you?"

The patrón touched the cane to the brim of his hat and said nothing, as if he had never laid eyes on her, as if she were a complete stranger of no special worth in his privileged world. Instantly, as if she had been yanked backward in time, she felt like a child again. He moved past her and down the hallway.

The old familiar frustration rose in her breast, and she whispered, "Damn you." In a louder voice, she called after him: "You don't even know who I am. Worse, you don't care!" She stood wringing her hands and then yelled, "I am your daughter—say it!"

He did not.

Fernando was sitting in the center of the loggia, watching her with an expression that said that, like Aba, he disapproved of her behavior. "I know," she muttered, "I know." The old cat ignored her and licked his paws. She reached down to scratch his head, and he took a wild bolo punch at her. She walked after her father.

He was sitting in the garden on a bench, looking perfectly relaxed, as if he had not a care in his life. His pet peacock, Sari, strolled over and stood nearby. Sister Ria sat on a bench opposite him and collected herself. When she had calmed sufficiently, she said, "I apologize, Father." Knowing he would be dead in eight days, Sister

Ria began to look at him differently. The sense of mistrust and loathing was still inside her, but there was something else, something she couldn't identify, something that made her study the lines of his face, his hands, to watch his breathing, the rise and fall of his narrow chest, the movement of his eyes.

He was wearing a strange assortment of her mother's jewelry pinned to the frock coat in various places, looking like some oddly decorated old soldier of the czars. For no apparent reason, he began poking the cane in the air, as if fencing with a phantom.

"It's a lovely morning, Father."

He hacked harder at the air.

"How are you feeling?"

He turned on the bench so that he was no longer facing her and continued his mad thrusts at vital parts of the firmament. Sister Ria straightened the folds of her habit and tried to think of a topic that might interest him. But all she could think of were the indignities of her life at the hands of this man.

As quickly as it had started, the patrón's mad assault on the heavens ceased, and he began feeding Sari handfuls of grain pulled from the pocket of his frock coat, holding the kernels in his palm and letting the large green bird peck at them. Fernando was interested in this development and hopped up on the bench next to Sister Ria to sit watching the enormous creature in wonder, his fur rising over his body and a strange rasping sound escaping from his throat.

"You shouldn't be hunting birds," she told him.

The old cat paid no attention, his one eye glued on the peacock.

Moments later, having settled on a strategy, he hopped down and began to slink toward the massive bird.

"Don't you dare," she snapped. The cat froze and flattened himself on the ground, his tail twitching back and forth like a lion's.

"Here, kitty, kitty," Don Maximiato said, chuckling, "get the birdie."

"Please don't encourage him."

The old man dusted his hands of the grain, then put his thumbs in his ears and fanned his fingers at her and fluttered his tongue. Sister Ria ignored him. Fernando ignored them both and was starting to slink over the ground again when Sari decided he'd had enough of the foolish tomcat. He flared his gigantic tail feathers and dropped his wings and scurried at the cat.

That was a mistake. While ten times Fernando's size, the bird had none of his speed, and Fernando was on his back in a flash, raking feathers from the poor creature at an alarming rate. He was just about to bite the back of Sari's neck when Sister Ria grabbed for him. The wily cat saw her coming and bolted off the bird into the garden.

The patrón was howling with laughter and stomping his feet. Sister Ria sat back down and watched him, slowly shaking her head. He had grown childish with age, but that did not displace the loathing she felt for him. She took a deep breath. "I told myself I was the reason for the way you treated me." She blew the air out of her lungs. "But I wasn't. I—"

Her father interrupted her with a ditty sung in falsetto. Knowing his little ballads were mostly bawdy tales about the anatomy of women, she turned and started back toward the house, humming to herself to block the sound of his voice.

She had refused supper and was lying under the covers of her bed, propped against the pillows, contemplating the open armoire in front of her. She could see her vests, the velvet and satin dress pants, the tall leather riding boots, the sombreros . . . all of it the fashion of a young Mexican male. She closed her eyes tight against the memories.

Aba was sitting on a wooden chair just inside the doorway, waiting silently on Sister Ria. The old woman had not moved or spoken in quite a while, and Sister Ria jumped when she said, "Eight days."

Sister Ria looked at her, opening her eyes wide and waiting for her to continue. She did not.

"There is nothing I can do," Sister Ria said.

Aba did not change her expression.

"Nothing."

"When I first saw you, Isadora, I thought you had come to save him."

"No."

Aba gazed at the floor. "You were always compassionate as a child—begging me to give food and money to the poor."

"Aba, listen to me."

The old servant looked up at her.

"If he won't tell me whether or not he murdered that woman, there is nothing I can do for him."

Aba continued to watch her. "Nothing you will do, you mean." She stood and left the room, pulling the door closed behind her.

"Wait," Sister Ria called. She hopped down from her bed and went out into the hallway. The servant was at the far end.

"Aba—" Sister Ria called.

The woman continued walking.

Sister Ria stood watching until Aba disappeared around a corner of the loggia. Sister Ria closed the door and sat on the edge of her bed, thinking about the impossibility of what Aba wanted from her. She shook her head. There was nothing she could do.

Nothing.

Sister Ria fixed her gaze on an old tintype sitting on the table beside her bed. It hadn't been there the night before. Curious, she picked it up. Her heart began to beat faster. She had been working in the fields the day it was taken. She stared at her clothing: leather pants and boots that rose to her knees, a dirty, sweat-stained shirt and vest. The tintype had been shot by a traveling photographer, but her father had composed it. And she was certain it was he who had placed it here in her room.

She couldn't take her eyes off of it. It represented all that had happened to her after the deaths of her mother and Ramón. She was standing beside Millie, who was posed sitting on a satin chair. Millie had turned sixteen that summer. She looked lovely, dressed in a dark high-necked velvet gown, one of their mother's silver tiaras in her long black hair, a painted Chinese fan in her hand.

At her father's direction, Isadora had placed her own hand, like a man, on her sister's shoulder. She stared at her face, holding her breath against an emotion she felt but didn't understand: an odd, twisted feeling somewhere between sadness and defiance.

She had been ordered in from the fields that afternoon.

He had forbidden her to wash.

She let her breath out slowly, continuing to scan her face in the tintype. She looked like one of the African warriors in the stereo-camera photos her father kept in the parlor: ghostlike, her skin coated in the heavy white cascara that the Mexican plasterers had mixed for her each morning. The thick paste was made from ground chicken bones and clay and pulverized root of agave, and when it dried, it froze her features in a ghoulish mask.

The paste had been her desperate attempt to hold on to the one shred of femininity he had not been able to take: her white skin. He had forced her to work in the harsh sun. The women in this desert country wore shawls and carried parasols, or simply stayed indoors during the hottest parts of the day to preserve the whiteness of their skin. Isadora could not. Now she tipped her head back and stared at the ceiling, blinking until the moisture was gone from her eyes. Then she looked back down at the ghoulish face in the picture. El Cadáver, the pueblo children had called her. She raised the photograph and kissed Millie. "Bless and miss you," she said. Then she laid the picture facedown on the nightstand, her thoughts returning to Aba's request.

"There is nothing I can do," she moaned.

Aba's words echoed in her head: *Nothing you will do.*

The morning was cool and moist, and Sister Ria was shivering when Aba opened the door to her small apartment at the rear of the hacienda. The old servant was still dressed. She looked tired. "Yes, child?"

Sister Ria just stared at her.

"Isadora?"

Sister Ria studied the lines of the old face for a time before she said, "I'll look into it."

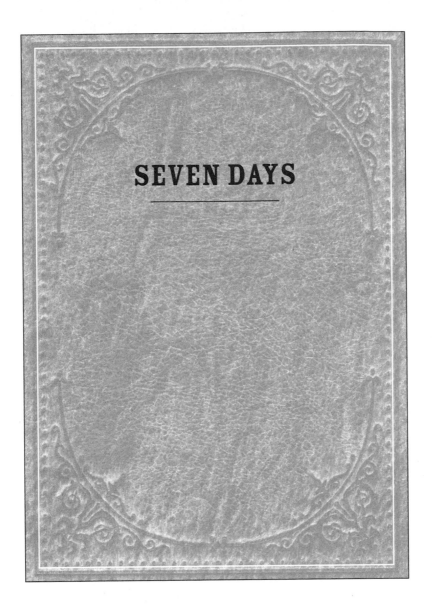

SEVEN DAYS

CHAPTER 5

SISTER RIA GAZED INTENTLY at the photograph of the young woman. She had been thinking about Dorothy Regal for so long, she felt she knew her. But the face of the girl in the picture looked different from the face Sister Ria had created in her mind—younger, more vulnerable. The girl was naked and child-awkward, lying on her back on the floor of a small room. Her throat had been cut. Her face was hard with death.

Sister Ria had seen the torn and decaying corpses of hundreds of young women—dead from childbirth, disease, and violence. She had prepared their bodies for burial and prayed over their souls. She had dressed them in their finest garments, and when they had nothing decent, she had begged clothing for them. She was familiar with the dead.

The voice of the man sitting across the desk from her brought Sister Ria back. "The night watchman found her the way you see her." He paused. "She was carrying a child. The fetus had been removed from her. We never found it."

"Who was she?" Sister Ria asked, not liking the man's impatient tone.

"Prostitute."

"Yes, but where did she come from? Did she have family? Other children who need taking care of?"

"Wasn't from here." He pointed at the photograph. "Handprints on her shoulders," he said, as if it might frighten Sister Ria, "whoever cut her throat held her down while she bled to death."

It did not.

"Are there other children who need taking care of, sir?" she pressed.

After a moment spent trying to figure out who this sweet-looking nun was who wasn't sickened by blood or easily scared, he shook his head no.

Sister Ria gently touched her fingers to the gaping wound in Dorothy Regal's belly, then drew an invisible cross over the stomach of the girl and another over Dorothy Regal's forehead. In a weak voice, she said, "She's naked."

"Prostitute," he repeated, as if this made her nakedness acceptable.

Sister Ria turned the photograph facedown, raising her eyes until she was looking over her reading glasses into the face of Raymond Hood, Los Angeles City's police chief. From another photograph in a wooden frame on his desk, it appeared that he had a staff of fifteen policemen. She remembered when the town had nothing more than an old Mexican who served part-time as sheriff—with a borrowed pistol—and part-time as carpenter. "She is naked," Sister Ria repeated firmly.

Hood was middle-aged, balding, with a long, thin, and deeply tanned face. He studied the features of this beautiful young nun, her face made all the more appealing by the perfect white headband framing it. Having watched her walk into his office, he knew that beneath the shapeless habit, her body was strong—tall and slender, with a nice way of moving—and the thought crossed his mind that a nunnery was a waste of her. He pushed himself up from his chair, stepped to a wooden filing cabinet, and took out a yellow envelope.

Sister Ria handed him the photograph. "Thank you," she said and took off her glasses. The room smelled of gun oil and burnt powder, and she figured there was a firing range somewhere in the building. "And my father had been with her?"

"We never found anyone who saw your father that night." By the light of the hurricane lamp on the desk, the man's eyes were tired-looking. "No witnesses. Nobody heard anything." He flipped through a stack of papers on his desk as if signaling that he had other, more important work waiting.

"Then I don't understand."

The old tomcat Fernando had stowed away in her wagon that morning and then taken to following her around town. At the moment, he was sharpening his claws on the heavy material of her habit. She nudged him with her foot. He bit her shoe and walked off.

Hood put down the papers and placed a large cardboard box on the desk. "We found these things in her room." He removed a black gaucho hat and a leather belt with a large gold buckle and set them on the desk.

Sister Ria was fighting her dislike of the man's arrogance. "Those are common—"

"Not with your father's initials stamped on them."

Sister Ria put her tiny spectacles back on and peered at the hat-band. The letters MRL were clearly visible in the leather. Maximiato Rialto Lugo. She pulled off her glasses and rubbed her eyes. "Did he confess? Make any statement?"

"No."

"Did he even know Dorothy Regal?"

Hood blew his nose in a handkerchief. "The woman rented her room from the Fiesta—she wasn't one of their girls."

She could feel her temper heating at the man's coldness. "Meaning?"

"Meaning we don't know who her clients were. But we have your father's things, so he was one of them."

"You figure, but you don't know."

"We have his things."

"Things that could have been placed there by anyone."

The man's face reddened. "We have his things," he repeated.

"What else, Mr. Hood?"

"Nothing."

With the finality of that pronouncement still ringing in the air, Fernando leaped agilely up onto Chief Hood's desk, sniffed a pile of official-looking papers, then curled up in a nicely tucked ball at the center of the ink blotter. The police chief, clearly not used to having feral cats turn his desk into a bed, looked annoyed. "That animal looks like he could carry the ringworm."

"He's just hurt," Sister Ria said.

Fernando yawned.

"He doesn't look to be in much pain to me, ma'am. What's his name?" There was no interest or affection in the question—it was more a practical statement, as if Hood were collecting information for an arrest report.

"Fern."

Hood raised his eyebrows slightly. "It's a male cat, Miss Lugo."

"Yes. But he's being punished."

The chief looked at her as if she might be a tad touched in the head, then he reached both hands to pick up the tom.

"I wouldn't do that," she said. "He isn't friendly."

The man stopped and sized up the large, mangy-looking animal with scars over most of his body, slumbering gallingly in the center of his desk. The chief pursed his lips, then seemed to have a brand-new thought: He slowly began to put the evidence items back into the cardboard box. Fernando was purring, the sound like a coarse file over iron.

Sister Ria focused on Hood's face. "Nobody knows whether my father even knew this woman. And there are no witnesses—just his hat and belt?"

Hood removed a sharp-bladed carving knife from the box and laid it in front of her. Sister Ria saw the Lugo family crest in the heavy silver handle. "On the floor next to the body," he said. She stared at the blade of the knife until the police chief said, "Anything else, Miss Lugo?"

"You've left him at home."

Fernando had risen from his brief nap and was stretching lazily in the center of the desk. Hood had his eyes on him. "Mexicans think your father is some sort of god," he said. "I don't need trouble with them. And something tells me he's not the running type."

Hood made a quick move to shove Fernando off the desk. But it wasn't quick enough, and Fernando sank his fangs into the police chief's hand, then sprang out the door.

Sister Ria stood and straightened her habit. "That's why he is being punished, sir." Hood was sucking on his hand. She wanted to kiss the old cat but figured it would be dangerous.

Sister Ria stood at the bottom of the jailhouse stairs, trying to think clearly and shivering in the hot morning air. All her life she had prided herself on being able to get her mind to work straight during times of trouble, but this time was different. Too much of her life was tied to this time. She pulled her shawl over her shoulders and gazed at the heavy three-story brick jail, squinting against the sunshine.

The building stood in the center of a large barren lot on the northwest corner of Spring and Jail streets, a squat, imposing structure so very serious and different-looking from the little converted adobe chicken coop that had served the same purpose when she was a girl. So much had changed.

Still, much remained the same.

She had driven into town that morning on the old dirt road that cut through the vineyard and fields, the look of things so familiar that the years of her absence had seemed to recede into the far distance. She had caught herself noticing small details—whether the tomatoes had been staked up to keep the fruit from rotting on the earth, whether the spring growth in the vineyard had been properly tied on the Guyot supports.

It had been her job to know these things.

He had made it her job. And he had punished her when she failed.

She took a deep breath and held it. His favorite had been to make her sleep in the field hands' quarters. It was frightening to spend the night surrounded by fifty or sixty sleeping men. One of the male servants was always assigned to watch over her, but that did not stop the rumors. The street children of the pueblo called her "the Cadáver whore of La Cienega."

She let out her breath slowly and thought back to her morning trip into town.

She had stopped at the side of the road and cautioned a group of young peones working the wooden irrigation gates—which controlled the flow of river water down the rows of guero chilies—that too much water would sweeten the crop, damaging it. Not certain they had understood, she had crawled down from her carriage and pulled up the heavy wooden gate, the muddy water flowing over her shoes and the hem of her robe. She had waded through the thick liquid and yanked up other gates to show them exactly how much water to let into the furrows.

The young men had been stunned at the sight of a woman, a nun no less, trudging around in the mud and water, muscling the irrigation gates, and instructing them in the proper watering of chile plants. But it was second nature to her. After the death of Ramón, she had been forced to learn to manage the vast lands and herds of La Cienega.

And she would never be the same.

She turned and walked down the brick path to the sidewalk, leaving the jail and the American business district behind her. Fernando trotted after her, meowing loudly about the fact that he had to walk all over town. "I didn't ask you to come along," she said, "but thank you for what you did in there." The old tom looked up at her, seemed to realize he wasn't going to persuade her, and quit wasting his breath.

She entered La Calle de los Mercados—Market Road—a wide dirt street lined on one side by sun-washed white adobe walls splashed over by pink and white sprays of wisteria and, on the other, by small shops open to the front. Immediately, she sensed the loneliness and shame she had always felt here after her mother and brother were gone. She pulled herself up to her full height and continued walking. Those days were gone. She would not be haunted by them.

People were moving through the little stores, and Mexican boys were scurrying in and out carrying trays of steaming coffee, hot chocolate, and fruit juices to their customers. When she lived here, this had been the only place to shop. She let her gaze drift over the powdery marketplace, finding it comforting to imagine herself a girl again, her childhood not yet destroyed, the town a small pueblo, her mother and brother still alive, her father not sentenced to death. She tensed at this last thought, balling her hands into fists until they began to throb.

I don't know what to do, Mother.

She shrugged off the sense of hopelessness and continued walking, the vendors beckoning her. There was an old Mexican woman sitting in the shade of a pastry stall, being fanned by a small Indian girl of six or seven. The child was barely able to pull the long rope that worked a complicated series of pulleys, causing the large canvas fan to wave back and forth over the pastries and the old woman, who sat drinking coffee from a small porcelain cup held daintily between her gnarled thumb and forefinger.

When Sister Ria stopped to look at the child, the woman motioned to her with a welcoming sweep of her hand over the mounds of food. "Sister of God, come inside my humble stall, please." The old woman grinned a toothless smile, covering her mouth with a withered hand. "These are heavenly dulces."

Sister Ria ignored her and stepped closer to the child. "Have you had a meal this morning?" she asked in Spanish. The girl in her tattered dress reminded Sister Ria of the orphans who wandered the streets and alleys of Poona, and the hollow sensation she always felt for them clutched like a hand at her throat.

Her thoughts turned to her sisters in India, and she smiled sadly. She had convinced them that, tired as they were, God wanted them to care for the orphans as well as the lepers. And when they were not working in the hospital, they would leave the lepers' village and beg food and money for the lost children in the city of Poona.

"Have you eaten?" she asked the little girl again.

The child stopped pulling on the rope and looked up and shook her head, her eyes burning into Sister Ria. The old woman stomped her foot, and the little girl jumped and started pulling on the rope again. Sister Ria took the rope from her hand and gave her a coin from the small bag Aba had left for her on the nightstand. "Go and have breakfast."

The girl hung back, nervously clutching the coin and staring at the old hag.

"Blessed Sister," the old woman said, "you have no right—"

Sister Ria leaned forward and placed a second coin in the woman's outstretched hand.

"But for this," the woman said, her eyes brightening, "she can take time for a meal." She waved the child away, lest Sister Ria take back her coin. The girl ran.

"She's a child, she should not be worked like a beast of burden," Sister Ria said, pulling on the rope to keep the fan waving and the flies off the pastries.

"It is how she lives; I care for her."

"I can see that," Sister Ria snapped, in no mood to be trifled with. Then she stopped herself and took a deep breath, reciting silently her vows to offer only tender mercy to others. She calmed some and said, "She is too small for the task."

The old woman shrugged. "Perhaps, but it is all that I have for her."

Sister Ria handed the rope to the woman and started to move away, but the old merchant clutched at her hand and moaned, "Sister, bless me with a prayer, for I am very old."

Sister Ria hesitated. "If you promise God to treat the child better."

The woman nodded. Sister Ria put her hand on the thin head and said, "Lord, bless this woman who has committed to you with her whole heart to take better care of this child—bless her with a long and healthy life."

Sister Ria stood looking down at the old woman for a moment before she said, "You must do what you have promised God. Do you understand?" The woman just stared at her. Sister Ria raised her eyebrows. Reluctantly, the old woman nodded, and Sister Ria made the sign of the cross on the mottled skin of her forehead.

Sister Ria walked on.

There were hatmakers, offering everything from handsome wide-brimmed Mexican sombreros to European fedoras and berets, and there were tailors, butchers, silversmiths, leather makers, confectioners, and potters. The gaudy colors, the sounds of shoppers and livestock mixing with the voices of the proprietors hawking their wares, brought back memories. Those before her mother's and brother's deaths were good—memories of her and Milagros dragging their poor governess, Leonora, up and down this dirt street in search of some grand prize of their imagination. But after her mother and brother were gone, all that changed, and the memories were of her father bringing her here mornings so that he could sit in the cafés and read the newspapers brought off the ships anchored in San Pedro harbor—the same mornings Milagros was taken by the nursemaids to Mercer's school to take *dance* lessons.

She had hated those mornings among the old men of the pueblo. He had always made her remove her hat at the tables. And no matter how many years she had come here, no matter how many times they had seen her, the men always gasped at the white paste and gawked at her shaved head. And the town children stood just outside the circle of men and taunted her. She was certain all of that had pleased him.

Sister Ria shrugged off the memory and told herself she was no longer a child.

She concentrated her thoughts on Milagros's dancing. Millie had been wonderful at it, had shown Isadora the steps for the waltz, the bolero, and the jota, the two of them practicing at night. Sister Ria swallowed hard. She had never danced with a man. She wondered what it would have been like. Something about that silly fact saddened her, and she closed her eyes and shook her head. None of it mattered now; she belonged to Christ.

She turned in a slow circle, trying to forget the past, focusing on the world around her. Slowly, the look and smells and sounds of the market seeped into her. At least some good pieces of the life she had known as a girl had survived and would exist no matter what happened to her or her father. She began moving again, passing by the fruiterers' stalls, carefully examining the quality of the oranges and lemons, peaches and apricots. It had been a good year for orchard crops. From the large size of the apricots and peaches, she estimated that there had been over eighteen inches of rain, when the average was somewhere closer to thirteen in a normal growing season. Yes, a good year.

She stopped and studied a cluster of grapes, her body tensing. She sensed she was being watched. It was the same sensation she had felt that first day in the hallway of the hacienda. But when she looked up, no one beyond the shopkeepers seemed to be paying her any mind. Then she saw a small man in a brown suit and black fedora standing and looking at her near the tinsmith's stall. But he turned away, and she was not certain he had been the one observing her.

She moved down the road and sat on an old wooden bench under the shade of a mulberry tree, gazing at the sights of the marketplace and wondering if the canasta and checkers players still came here in the afternoons to test their skills. Not far down the road, in an empty lot, were a number of Mexican men and women sitting in a row like schoolchildren in stiff-backed chairs, listening to a young man with glasses in a clean white shirt reading the newspaper out loud. She smiled in recognition—things hadn't changed that much. There was still a Spanish feel to the pueblo, in spite of the Americanos.

The market was filling up with people. The Mexican men were, for the most part, laborers dressed in rough cotton clothes; the women wore bright dresses, shawls, and straw hats. There were also Chinese women in colorful, tight knee-length silk dresses that were split daringly up the side, with beautiful paper parasols open on their shoulders as protection from the sun. Then there were the Americans and Europeans, fairly large numbers of them for the hour, the women wearing high-collared dresses and hats with long silk ribbon ties and white gloves. Sister Ria stretched the tenseness from her shoulders. Where was Milagros? She had always been so close to their father. Why had she not come?

It made no sense.

✝

The brothel where Dorothy Regal had been murdered stood in bright morning sunlight at the end of a small bricked alleyway known as Strand's Road. Sister Ria was standing at the bottom of a flight of wooden stairs that ran up the side of the building, hesitating and uncertain why. She had witnessed hundreds of death chambers.

There was no one around, and no sounds came from inside the building. The sign on the rope at the bottom of the stairs finally stiffened her resolve.

Keep Out
By Order of the Department of Police
City of Los Angeles

Something about the sign seemed as cold as Chief Hood. She quickly ducked under the rope, raising the hem of her robe and trotting defiantly up the stairs. Fernando bounded up the wooden steps behind her. She tried the door.

Open.

She stepped inside, and the old cat shot through the opening before she shut the door. It was dark, and Sister Ria pulled some wallpaper off the window glass and let her eyes adjust to the morning shadows. The room was small and cheap and filled with the heavy smell of human sweat and perfume. She glanced at the neatly made bed and tried to keep from thinking what had gone on here. Then she looked down at the floor and jumped.

They had not cleaned up the blood, and she could see the outline of Dorothy Regal's head and shoulders clearly in the brown stain. She brought a hand to her throat. The girl had been even smaller than she'd appeared in Hood's photograph, the span of her shoulders childlike. "You poor thing," Sister Ria whispered. She crossed herself and knelt down beside the bloodstain and clasped her hands. Though she had witnessed death in a myriad of forms, she knew she would never get used to it—that each time it would tear away a piece of her heart. Fernando sniffed at the edges of the stain.

As she was praying, Sister Ria reached down for her wooden crucifix that hung on the cincture around her waist. Her hand groped for it before she realized it was not there. She pulled the cord up in front of her face. It had been cut; the crucifix was gone. He must have done it while she was asleep in the hallway. "Damn you," she muttered and then said, "Forgive me, Lord," and returned to her prayer for Dorothy.

Sister Ria spent a long time in the room, looking around at the small cramped compartment with its iron bed, table and chair, brass kerosene lamp. She did not know what to do next. She had searched every inch of it and then hunted through a stack of Dorothy's papers in a box on the table, mostly playbills from local theaters. She had found only one thing that seemed worth keeping: a small slip of paper that had been torn from a writing tablet. It had been dropped on the floor.

She unfolded it and read the printed words—*Brown cutaway*—written in a blue ink. Lower down the small slip was penciled the word *Curandera*—female healer. Had the dead woman been sick? The only healer Sister Ria could remember was an ancient hag by the name of Nachita, rumored to have been the oldest woman in the world. Sister Ria had no idea what the words might mean. But she held on to the paper. The police appeared to have removed everything else from this small, dirty room filled with sadness and lost dreams. Still, she lingered. Did she want to pray once more? Perhaps that was it.

She saw it as she was kneeling.

It was barely visible under the edge of the pillow: the corner of a book. Sister Ria picked it up: *The Poems of Alfred, Lord Tennyson,* Volume II. She rubbed her fingertips over the soft leather binding and stared at the gold letters. It was a small pocket edition of love poems in a beautiful leather cover. Something about it did not make sense. It was expensive. It did not fit in this cheap room. If Dorothy Regal had loved Tennyson, there were canvas- or paper-covered editions.

Sister Ria shook her head. That wasn't fair, she told herself. Perhaps this was Dorothy Regal's only way to touch something fine and good in her sad life. Sister Ria thumbed through the book. There was no inscription, no initials of ownership, nothing. She placed the piece of paper inside the little book, slipped them both into the pocket of her robe, and began to carefully move through the apartment again. This time she knew what she was looking for: Volume I.

It was not there.

Lord, please help me.

Sister Ria stood waiting for some sign, some inclination in her heart. When none came, when the frustration of having been drawn into this futile search for answers she was certain would lead nowhere soared inside her head, she snapped, "I can't help him."

CHAPTER 6

SISTER RIA WAS SEARCHING the house for her father. He had left discarded sketches in the central courtyard; others had been tossed away near the two iron lions guarding the path to the stables, and still others were strewn over the floor of the loggia.

She found him in the small sitting room next to the library, stretched out on a méridienne, sketching furiously on a stack of papers. His large wooden painting easel was set up nearby. She pulled a chair close and sat facing him. He was dressed as a Catholic priest, in a bone-white surplice with a purple sash tied around his waist and a large silver crucifix dangling from a heavy chain around his neck. Strange as it seemed, he was wearing a Jewish yarmulke on his head. Though she had intentionally scraped the chair over the tile floor, he did not look up at her.

She studied his face. He had aged badly. The skin around his mouth and eyes was sagging and deeply wrinkled, and he had a sickly sallow cast. His eyebrows were flecked with silver, his hair thin to the point where she could see scalp. But there was something about him—the essence of him—that had not changed. She saw it in the expression in his eyes, a mixture of energy and fire.

"Father—"

He did not look up.

When he worked at his sketching and painting, no one dared to disturb him. Aba knew to keep the servants quietly occupied in other parts of the hacienda and to turn visitors away. When he had finished working, he would retire to his room or the gardens. Sister Ria cleared her throat loudly. She didn't care what he demanded. As if in response, he crumpled a sheet of paper, tossed it to the floor, and went back to sketching.

"Did you kill that girl?" she asked.

He looked up at her, eyebrows slightly raised. "What girl?"

She stood over him, shaking her head. "Father, please do not play games. The girl they are going to execute you for killing. Did you kill her?"

"I thought you had come for an apology for your little hurts. I liked you so much better then. You've become tiresome."

"I don't care what I've become. I want to know if you killed Dorothy Regal."

He tipped back his head and scanned the ceiling of the room, as if searching for the small lizards that sometimes scaled the walls. Then he seemed to remember that she was standing in front of him, and he looked at her. "I will trade you your robe for a seventeenth-century satin cloak with jabot and wide sleeves." He examined her vestments with an appraising eye, then continued, "But only if you include your headpiece—what is it called?"

"It's called a wimple."

"Will you include it?"

"I do not want one of your silly outfits."

"Then may I borrow yours?"

"No. You may not. But I do want you to return my crucifix—the wooden crucifix you stole," she said, holding up the frayed end of her cincture. "And I want you to answer me about the woman."

"It is a very nice satin cloak."

"I don't care," she mumbled.

She heard the sound of children playing somewhere in the gardens, and her thoughts drifted. She'd had only one friend besides Millie: Elsie. She bit at her lip. She had been shunned because of him, because of the cascara, and because he had turned her into a girl who wore men's clothing and worked among them, sometimes staying with them in their sleeping places.

Weeks before her twelfth birthday, she had sent out two dozen handwritten invitations to the children of the old pueblo families—the Sepulvedas, the Duartes, the Picos—inviting them to celebrate with her. The house was decorated with colored papers and flowers, and cakes and sweet drinks prepared. The party was to start at noon. Isadora waited to greet her guests on the veranda. She waited until Aba came and stood beside her chair. Neither of them spoke. Each time a rider or coach arrived, Aba would walk out and accept the note of condolence, thanking the messenger for the family's great kindness.

They waited late into the night. Often, as she lay in the dark of the convent feeling alone, Isadora would remember Aba's silent vigil with her—the quiet strength and fierce loyalty of the servant woman—as one of the kindest things that had ever been done for her.

No one came to her party.

Thus the day that she was invited to the Banning hacienda to celebrate the fourteenth birthday of Celeste Banning was tremendously exciting. What Isadora did not know was that Aba had spoken to the Bannings' head servant, who in turn had spoken to Mrs. Banning, telling her that it would be a kind and generous act for a lonely child. And so Isadora Lugo was invited to Celeste Banning's birthday party with some twenty-five other children of local well-to-do Mexican families.

While her father allowed her to attend only if she wore pants, Millie had loaned her a beautiful silk blouse with a frilly laced collar.

It was a lovely spring day, the fields aflame with flowing seas of golden poppies, the sky cloudless, the air warm but not hot. The children were playing a tag game with green ribbons in the graveled front yard of the Banning hacienda. While standoffish, Celeste and her young guests had treated Isadora decently, including her in their games, and if they'd talked about her, they had done it discreetly. They were all dressed in their finest, the girls in sundresses and bonnets with long ribbons and white gloves, and the boys—as well as Isadora—wearing sombreros, short jackets, and fine pants. Isadora was "it," and she stood in the center of the sunlit square with her eyes closed, counting out loud, as the rules required.

When she opened her eyes, she was surprised to see the governesses herding the other children quickly into the hacienda, staring back over their shoulders at something behind Isadora. She turned and looked. It was the first time she had ever seen him masquerade outside of La Cienega, and she wanted to run and never stop running.

The patrón was sitting on a beautiful Arabian stallion, wearing a black satin woman's riding habit with a feathered top hat and veil, white waistcoat, and red cravat, his skirt-covered bare leg draped over the pommel hook of a woman's sidesaddle. "Do you like my outfit?" he asked, smiling down at her.

The cruel whispers and giggling began again . . .

Sister Ria pushed aside the memory and focused her eyes hard on her father. He had gone back to his sketching.

"Much has been neglected by you," he said, expertly smearing charcoal over the paper with his palm.

She shook her head. "No. This isn't about me. I need to know. Did you kill that girl?"

"Have you come to disturb my work?"

"No. I came because of Mother. Now, tell me, are you a murderer?"

Don Maximiato was staring at the ceiling again. Then he looked at her. "You were never one to stick with a task."

"How dare you!"

"This is a sanctuary. Please keep your voice down."

"This is not a sanctuary. You are not a priest. You are simply mad."

"I am."

"You are what? Mad?"

"A holy man."

"You forget that I am your daughter. I grew up in this house. I know you."

He stared at her.

"You take lovers," she said. "What kind of holy man takes lovers?"

"Not lovers, whores."

"Whatever. You are not a holy man."

He appeared to drift into sleep.

With fear and frustration building inside her, Sister Ria turned and went to his easel and took a brush, dabbing it into a jar of black paint. Then she walked to a nearby wall and brushed a large number seven on the stark white plaster. She turned and faced him. Her hands were trembling. "Perhaps that will help you—you have seven days left of life. Do you understand? Seven days!"

He had opened his eyes and was looking down at his papers again. "Why does the Almighty hide?" he asked. "Is He ashamed of His creation?"

"Please just answer me. Did you kill Dorothy Regal?"

He was suddenly as excited as a child. "Soon God will take me in His embrace."

She stood up slowly, bracing herself on the arm of the chair, moving with great difficulty. "Yes, Father, very soon," she said softly. "I pray so."

She started to leave the room, then noticed that she had gotten paint on her hand. She went back and picked up the paper he had tossed on the floor and opened it up. She froze. It was the same woman she had seen in the police photograph—Dorothy Regal. He had sketched Dorothy Regal's head and shoulders, and the dead girl was smiling. Sister Ria balled the paper in her hand, squeezing it until her knuckles were white, and threw it at him, the paper bouncing off his head. He didn't flinch. She was sobbing without sound. Then she heard two sharp raps on the heavy tile floor and turned and saw Aba standing in the doorway.

CHAPTER 7

THE AFTERNOON LIGHT was creating a sepia tone on the towering walls of the hacienda's library, making the room, with its long
reading table and lacquered globes, look like an old tintype. Fernando was batting a small white feather up and down the length of
the table. Sister Ria took a deep breath and gazed at the floor-to-
ceiling bookshelves surrounding her. Like her father's life, they had
no order to them—over a hundred years of Lugo family records and
reading material. She shook her head. It didn't matter. She had to
concentrate, had to know if the companion volume of Tennyson was
here. Sister Ria stopped and turned in a full circle; the same feeling
of being watched that she'd felt before flowed over her. The room
was empty. She turned back to the books. Her imagination was getting out of control. She had to stop it.

She climbed to the top of the library ladder and began to run her
fingertips over the titles. Finished with the first row, she moved
down a step and did the same to the second. Earlier, while he was in
the garden painting, she had quickly searched his cluttered bedroom

and found nothing. She had gone through the other rooms of the hacienda. Again, nothing.

She was inching her way down the rows of books when her eyes locked on a thin volume. She pulled it out. Unlike the others, it had been dusted recently. Her heart was starting to race. *The Anatomy of Human Dissection.*

"Is there a specific book you are searching for?" Aba asked.

Sister Ria jumped and turned on the ladder, feeling like she'd been caught stealing. "Pardon?" she said, sliding the book back into its place on the shelf.

"A book," Aba said, shooing Fernando off the table and leaning on her cane, "is there a specific one that I can find for you?"

"No," Sister Ria said, trying to collect herself. "I'm just looking them over. Is that a problem, Aba?"

The old woman stiffened at the remark. "None whatsoever, Isadora. This is your home. You may do as you wish. The problem lies in your behavior toward your father."

Sister Ria began to search the titles again. "I apologize."

"You don't mean that, child. So don't say it to me."

Sister Ria stared at the wall of books and tried to regain her composure. Finally she said, "There is one book I'd like to find. It's a small leather-bound volume of Tennyson poems. Have you seen it?"

"No," Aba said, "I have not."

Sister Ria was still facing the shelves when she continued, "He sketched the face of the dead woman—Dorothy Regal."

"He sketches many things. He is interested in many things."

"In dead women?"

"I do not care for your insinuation, Isadora."

Sister Ria was suddenly angry. She pulled the dissection book from the shelf and held it down to Aba.

"Your insolence is not becoming to the daughter of the patrón," Aba said, glancing at the book. "He has always been a student of the human body. He is an artist."

"Where was he on the night of her death?"

"I'm sure he was in his room."

"Did you see him there?"

"You know that I do not enter the patrón's quarters after he has retired for the night."

"So you don't know?"

"I know the patrón." Aba cocked her head and squinted at Sister Ria. "Do you not, child?"

"No," Sister Ria said, "I do not."

CHAPTER 8

THE RESTAURANT was French and built around a handsome courtyard of fine trees and thick beds of yellow lilies, night-blooming jasmine, white phlox, and spires of deep pink foxglove. It was late evening, and the colored lanterns strung through the branches of the trees cast a romantic glow over the grounds. The dining room with its perfectly clean white tablecloths and wavering candlelight opened onto this square; the air smelled of jasmine mixed with the ever present odor of sage from the hills. The restaurant was on the ground floor of the Pico Hotel, across the street from the town plaza.

Sister Ria was waiting for the young newspaper editor, Clemente Rojo, whom she had spoken to that morning in the offices of the Mexican newspaper *La Verdad*. The editor was to join her for dinner. She replayed the afternoon over and over in her mind. She had learned nothing. Volume I was not in the hacienda—all she had found was the book on surgical procedures.

The muscles of her back tightened. The book on dissection had been recently handled, and both of Dorothy Regal's carotid arteries had been severed by a deep arcing cut, the woman neatly gutted, her child sliced from her womb. Not hacked, sliced. Sister Ria bit down on her lip and clenched her hands as if she were going to hit something.

Aba is right. Having a book on dissection did not make him a murderer. He was an artist, and artists studied the human body. Leonardo da Vinci had paid grave robbers to bring him fresh corpses to examine.

Not certain whether she should be comforted by this last thought, Sister Ria smoothed a pure white napkin over her lap, running her fingertips across the soft material. In another room, someone was playing most beautifully the Largo from "Winter" by Vivaldi on a harp, the lilting notes drifting softly on the air. Sister Ria's table was on the veranda, and she was drinking chilled water and watching the full moon rising over the distant San Gabriel Mountains and thinking about the girl's face in Don Maximiato's drawing, wondering if he could possibly be mad enough to murder. Aba had told her that Dorothy Regal's death photograph had run in the newspapers for weeks during the trial; the servant was certain that was where the patrón had seen it. Sister Ria shivered and forced her thoughts on.

The evening air felt brisk and clean. She might be sitting in a restaurant in any fine hotel in Europe. It was amazing, this transformation of the pueblo. She took a sip of her water. Then guilt struck her.

Her fellow sisters would have sat this night at the long convent table in the gray stone refectory, drinking cheap wine with their meager meal because neither the village's nor the city's water was fit to drink. What was she doing, dressed in this lovely new habit of fine light linen cloth that Aba had had sewn for her, drinking water with crystals of ice floating in it, awaiting a meal whose cost would provide a year of food for a family in Poona? She had vowed to live as the poor lived, not in the luxury of her former life. Was she ready to renounce her sacred vows? She stiffened at the thought.

"Are you okay?" Clemente Rojo asked. He stood at the edge of the table.

"Yes, I'm fine," she said, releasing her grip on the tablecloth, "just tired."

"Tired, perhaps—but you look lovely, Sister," he said, bowing slightly.

She reddened, wondering if she would ever get used to being openly stared at or commented on by men. "It is good to see you again, Mr. Rojo."

"Clemente, please," he said. "Where is Happy?"

"Pardon?"

"Happy Fernando. I expected to see him curled around the salt shaker."

She laughed. The old cat had taken a nap in the center of the young editor's desk that morning, just as he had on Chief Hood's. She guessed he liked desks, or perhaps he just liked to annoy people. It was probably the latter.

"He asked me to send his regrets—he did not have proper attire."

Clemente smiled. "Our loss."

Clemente Rojo didn't look any older than she was, though he carried himself like an old man, with an almost humorous seriousness that spoke of grave concerns and heavy responsibilities. Small and thin, he wore heavy steel-framed glasses that he periodically pushed up his nose as though they had been borrowed from someone else.

Unlike the other men in the restaurant, most of whom were Americans or Europeans, Clemente was dressed in a beautifully embroidered Mexican short-waisted jacket in black velvet and tight-fitting pantaloons that flared over a pair of handsome black dress boots. The same style of clothing she had once worn. She reached across the table and handed him the stack of newspaper editorials on the trial of her father that he had given her that morning. "Thank you for these."

"Useful?"

"Very." She paused. "But unfortunately, I don't have any real answers about what happened that night."

"How was your meeting with Chief Hood?"

"The police believe that everything they found points to my father."

Clemente watched her for a moment. "And you don't?"

"Nothing I've seen or heard proves my father's guilt." She took a sip of water. "I am not saying he's innocent, I'm just saying they didn't have enough to convict him. Aside from some of his possessions, they have nothing—no convincing explanation for why he would have done it, no witness who saw him with the woman the night she was murdered. They don't even know whether or not he knew her. And more to the point, their investigation appears to have been very superficial."

Clemente picked up the piece of paper listing the restaurant's wines, waiting for her to continue.

She hesitated but could see no reason not to tell him. "I went to her room today. I found a book there under her pillow. The police hadn't even stripped her bed." She paused. "If they hadn't even bothered to look in her bed—in a room that tiny—how thorough could their search have been?"

Clemente didn't comment on the police work; he just looked over the edge of the wine list at her. "A book—why would that be important?"

"I don't believe it belonged to her. It was a book of Tennyson poems, expensive leather-bound, one of two volumes."

"And you think it belonged to the killer?"

"I don't know. All I know is that the police should have found it—and at least questioned who it belonged to."

Clemente pursed his lips and sat thinking. "Volume one or volume two?"

She evaded the question, staring down at her hands on the table; she wasn't certain why. When she looked back up, the editor was studying the wine list.

"You're smart not to believe all that Hood tells you," he said finally, his eyes still fixed on the page.

She tensed. "Why is that, sir?"

"His department is corrupt."

Sister Ria felt the muscles across her shoulders tighten even more. She continued to stare at Clemente. "Are you saying he framed my father?"

"No. Just that he is capable of it."

They spent the next few minutes talking about the poor condition of law enforcement in the city of Los Angeles, Hood and his department, injustices committed against the Mexicans and Chinese in town. The more Clemente talked, the more Sister Ria liked the young editor, finding his conversation candidly fresh and interesting. But it was not helping her.

"You are not saying that he framed my father?"

"No. I know nothing like that. Just that Hood doesn't care much for Mexicans, which would explain why—once they found your father's clothes—the police stopped investigating Dorothy Regal's murder."

Clemente went back to studying the wines. Finally, he placed the page on the table. "He is a very odd man, your father."

Sister Ria nodded.

"One day he arrived in court dressed like a pirate, with a tri-cornered hat and an eye patch and knee pants, stockings and brass-buckled shoes." He waited. "Another day he came dressed like a woman one would expect to see at the Moulin Rouge."

None of this surprised Sister Ria.

"Did he always—"

"Dress so exotically?" she offered.

"Yes."

"Always," she said, shaking her head at the lunacy of a man on trial for his life behaving in this way. But then neither the trial nor the people conducting it meant anything to him. No one, she knew, meant anything to him.

She least of all.

"Though of an odd nature," Clemente resumed, his voice respectful, "your father nevertheless is considered a saint to the poor Mexicans of Los Angeles for all that he has done."

"And what is that, sir?" she asked, coldness in her voice.

Clemente looked at her as if surprised that she didn't know. "He has stood up for them. Stood up against all that the Americans have done to them."

Sister Ria shook her head slowly. "They sell sainthood cheaply," she said.

Clemente ignored the comment.

After their dinner, Sister Ria left the young newspaperman inside the restaurant, interviewing a Chicago businessman who had just arrived in town. She had learned interesting details from Clemente but nothing new, nothing other than speculation about the death of Dorothy Regal. And she remained as convinced as ever of her father's guilt. The tragedy, she told herself, was that he would be executed without proof that he was a murderer. Once again, he would escape responsibility for his actions.

She walked out of the hotel and crossed the street to the old plaza gardens. The night sky was sprayed with flecks of gold across a vast black wash. She knelt on the grass and tipped her head up at the stars and prayed for an answer. Any answer that would put an end to the torrent of questions flooding through her mind.

Nothing came to her. She struggled to her feet and made her way down a brick path, her habit snagging on the branches growing over the walk, wandering trancelike through the maze of footpaths that ran through stands of overgrown bushes and trees.

She pushed open a wooden gate and moved past a flush of pink oleanders and towering, sharp-bladed agave plants. Peach trees, heavy with fruit, lined the other side of the walkway; the straight lines of the path were softened by the masses of flowers that spilled over the bricks. She continued walking without any sense of direction.

The night was cool, and she pulled her shawl tighter around her shoulders. Then she stopped and stood in the darkness. When she finally started moving again, she was listening closely to the night, staring at the bricks beneath her feet. Someone was walking in the garden with her, matching his or her steps to hers.

She turned around. The path behind her was empty. But she sensed something in the darkness and turned back and started quickly away, trying to determine where she should head.

She had moved only a short distance when she heard the sound again: quick, careful footsteps. She stopped. The sound stopped. That was all it took. Yanking her veil over her face to mask the white of her headband, she hurriedly wormed her way deep into the bushes beside the path.

She held her breath and waited.

Nothing. Knowing that any movement would be seen, she froze

and squinted through the gauzelike screen of cloth, vegetation, and shadows. There was no one on the path. Ten minutes. Still nothing. Perhaps she had only imagined the sound. Nothing seemed out of place in the gardens or the night. As she was getting ready to leave her hiding place, something stirred the bushes behind her, and a hand slid over her mouth.

In the midst of her rising fright came the whispered words: "Do you know me, nun?"

Sister Ria clamped down on the air in her throat and held it and shook her head.

"Have you not sinned?"

"Yes," she stammered.

"I thought so," the voice whispered in her ear.

Panic surging in her like waves against a seawall, she whirled to throw a punch, then froze, fighting off a yell of surprise. "Milagros?"

Her sister was bent over with laughter.

CHAPTER 9

"I CAN'T BELIEVE IT'S YOU," Sister Ria said, staring at her sister's face in the soft yellow lamplight of the hotel room. "How did you find me?"

Milagros was sitting in a chair. "I saw Father's carriage on the street and was looking for him when I came upon a nun praying like the holy Madonna in the gardens." She laughed softly. "I figured it could only be my little sister, Izzie."

Studying Millie in the lamplight, Sister Ria realized how much she missed her. Throughout those awful years, her sister had always been there for her, had stood shoulder to shoulder with her whenever the pueblo's street boys teased and bullied her, throwing rocks and taunting her and challenging her to fistfights. She and Milagros had lost most of the battles, but they never ran, a fact that drove their young governess, Leonora, frantic. Milagros had also taken her part with their father, bravely standing up to the man's wrath, even as a child.

Sister Ria leaned forward and kissed the top of Milagros's head. "You were always my heroine."

Milagros smiled sadly. "Las Animas Perdidas—the Lost Souls."

"Yes," Sister Ria said, remembering the game they had loved. Milagros had changed into a nightgown and satin robe, her hair in a soft pompadour that showed off her magnificent face with its delicate bone structure, wide eyes, full lips. "You were La Conquistadora, Our Lady of Victory," Sister Ria continued, "and I was your trusted helper Santa Osita—Saint Little Bear. You wore that wonderful golden cape we stole from Father."

She watched Milagros brush away a gleaming black strand of hair. As usual, Millie put up a good front, smiling through her sadness. Sister Ria continued in a soft voice, "I present the Grand Conquistadora, *pray for her soul.*" She tipped her head back and squinted at the ceiling. "And we had a flower."

"La Rosa de Castilla."

"Yes. Whenever you saved someone, I would present you with La Rosa de Castilla."

They held each other and cried, the years dropping away.

"Milagros, thank God you are here," Sister Ria whispered. Her older sister had always been so capable. Sister Ria's chest tightened. Only once had she ever known Millie to panic.

Years ago, as children, they had slipped away from their nurse-maids, who were taking their midday rest on the veranda. Having successfully escaped, they gathered their costumes and ran to play at the large brick cistern behind the horse barn. It was a perfect place for their favorite version of La Conquistadora: La Pirata. They had brought Emilia, the five-year-old daughter of the servant Rosa, to play the part

*of El Niño Perdido—the Lost Boy. And now Emilia was standing out
on the center of the boardwalk that spanned the dark waters, a rope tied
around her waist because she could not swim, the other end held by Milagros, the little girl looking dutifully frightened and ready to be saved by
the great Conquistadora. Emilia had played the role many times and
loved it every bit as much as the sisters did. Then the frown left the little
girl's face, and she started laughing and clapping her hands together.*

"Silencio," Isadora said, "you must look scared."

*"Yes," Milagros added, "you are about to walk the ship's plank to a
watery death."*

*Emilia looked appropriately solemn again and took a careful step
forward.*

*"Wait," Isadora said, stopping the game and crawling down the
cistern's ladder, running to cut a rose from the garden that she could
present to La Conquistadora after she had saved the child. For Isadora,
it was always the best part of the game, this solemn ceremony that hon-
ored the sister she loved so dearly.*

*When she climbed back up onto the brick wall of the cistern,
Emilia was no longer on the plank. The safety rope was gone as well.
Milagros just stood and stared down at the dark waters.*

*Milagros said the girl had slipped on the wet plank and fallen into
the water. And she had panicked and dropped the rope. The patrón
paid Emilia's family compassion money.*

Milagros was leaning back now in the chair, nervously inhaling
from a cigarette in a silver holder, her features locked in an expression of blunt panic. Sister Ria knelt and grasped her hand.

A smile softened Milagros's face. She pulled her hand free and slowly stroked her sister's cheek. "I still can't believe you are a nun—little Santa Osita who stole many hundreds of galletas dulces—cookies—from the poor bakers. Surely you will go to hell for that." The smile left her face, replaced by a deep sadness.

Sister Ria stood and kissed the top of her sister's head again. Her gaze wandered to an open closet and a rack of expensive clothes; close by was a pile of silk undergarments—the fine trappings of the wife of a San Francisco banker. "You've been here awhile," she said.

"Yes. Hounding judges, politicians, police—anybody who might know something about that night." Milagros wrapped her arms around her middle as if her stomach hurt.

"You haven't seen Father?"

"I've had to be strong. Seeing him would break my heart."

Sister Ria watched Milagros for a time before she said, "I went to her room today."

"Whose room?"

"Dorothy Regal's. Have you seen it?"

Milagros shook her head.

"It's just a single room above a brothel. The poor child. She had nothing."

"He didn't kill her."

"I found a book—" Sister Ria paused. "A leather-bound book, the second volume of Tennyson's love poems. I don't think it was hers. It might belong to her killer."

Milagros was gazing at the floor.

"I searched the library at La Cienega for the first volume. It wasn't there."

"Because he didn't kill her." Milagros looked exhausted.

Sister Ria continued talking. She had to get these things out. "There was a slip of paper on her table with writing on it that said *Brown cutaway*. And, on the bottom, *Curandera*. Does that make any sense to you?"

Milagros shook her head. "The curandera could be Nachita, that old beggar woman who pretended to be a healer and diviner. The one the mission priests condemned as a witch."

Sister Ria nodded. "I thought of her. She can't still be alive, can she?"

Milagros shrugged. "Father didn't kill that woman."

"I wish I could be so certain."

Compassion altered Milagros's features. "Those things happened to you a long time ago, Izzie. You can't keep condemning him."

"It's more than that," Sister Ria said, kneeling before her sister again, placing her hands on both sides of Milagros's head. "Milagros, listen to me."

Their eyes met.

"He's worse than when we were children."

"He didn't do it."

"Millie, he's not right."

"He didn't do it," Milagros snapped.

"How can you be so sure?"

Milagros hesitated. "Because I know who did."

Sister Ria didn't speak immediately. She just stared at her sister's eyes. Finally, she said, "Millie? What are you saying?"

"Father didn't kill her. Someone else did."

Sister Ria studied Millie's face, fighting the apprehension in her chest. "Who?"

"No, Izzie."

"What do you mean, no? Tell me who."

"I don't want you involved."

"Tell me."

"I'm not going to tell you. It is too dangerous."

"Tell me!" Sister Ria screamed.

"All right. Two men. Are you satisfied?"

"What men?"

Milagros rubbed her forehead, and her eyes moved slowly over her sister's face. "They planned it a year ago."

"Why?"

"To get rid of Father—"

"Why would they want to get rid of Father?"

"Because they're going bankrupt."

"What does that have to do with Father?"

"He is the only person who can save them."

"Millie, none of this makes sense."

"Three years ago these men won the city of Los Angeles's street-lamp contract. They were buying local tar to burn as fuel, but it caused a noxious cloud to spread over the town, and the city banned its use. Now they have to ship coal in from Australia, and they're going broke." Milagros picked up the cigarette in the holder and puffed anxiously until the ash turned orange.

Confusion deepened on Sister Ria's face. "I still don't see what that has to do with Father."

"I'll tell you if you promise to leave Los Angeles."

"Millie!"

"Promise you'll think about leaving."

"No. Now tell me."

"Geologists say there is coal under the water at La Brea Hoya."

Sister Ria frowned. La Brea Hoya—the tar pit—was a swamp marsh on the eastern edge of La Cienega. The oily waters were considered worthless except for the gummy tar that bubbled to the surface and was used to caulk barrels and roofs.

Milagros took another nervous draw on her cigarette. "They offered Father fifty thousand dollars for mining rights on five acres. Then seventy-five. But you know Papa. He wouldn't sell. Not at any price." She was staring at a spot between her shoes. "And so they framed him to get rid of him."

Sister Ria stood and paced back and forth in front of her sister. "Why didn't you tell the police?"

"I did, and they laughed."

Sister Ria thought of her conversation with Clemente Rojo. The muscle beneath her eye began to twitch. "Father drew Dorothy Regal's picture this afternoon," she said weakly.

Milagros's voice rose in frustration. "Father didn't kill her, Izzie."

She stopped and collected herself. "They sent a man to me last week. I told him I knew what they had done, that I wouldn't sell, either." She looked up at her sister. "They'll try to kill me now."

"Milagros, stop it—"

"And now you're here, Izzie." The words seemed to float in the room.

Sister Ria thought of the bloody cross on the wall of her bedroom and the odd sensation of being watched at the hacienda and again in the marketplace. But she quickly shoved these aside, certain in her heart that her father had not only killed the rooster in her room, he had also killed Dorothy Regal.

"Milagros . . ."

Milagros shut her eyes and held up her hands to stop her sister from saying anything more. "These men are desperate. You have to understand that. You have to be frightened of them."

Sister Ria began to pace again. When she stopped, she was standing by a small desk beneath the front window. She rubbed the edge of a silver frame containing a photograph of Milagros and her husband, Robert Sullivan. Milagros had met him twelve years before at a dinner party while she was attending Mrs. Andre's Finishing School in San Francisco. She had married him one month later. Sister Ria had never met him. Milagros had never brought him home. Sister Ria didn't blame her. Their home life and father were not easily explained to strangers. She jumped when Milagros touched her shoulder.

Milagros hugged her from behind and then let her go and lit another cigarette. "Go back to Spain. Or India. Anywhere. Just go."

"And leave you?"

"I'm leaving as well—to see the governor in Sacramento and try to get a stay of execution. It's not safe here any longer." Milagros wiped her face with her hand, her eyes narrowing as she fought the tears. "Then I'll go home to San Francisco. I've asked my husband to hire new detectives. I'm afraid the ones here have been bought off." She looked at her sister. "Please, Izzie."

Sister Ria pulled herself up to her full height and turned to her sister. "Millie, give me their names."

"Just leave."

"No."

"You must go, Izzie."

"Their names, Millie."

✝

The convent at Poona seemed so distant, Sister Ria wondered if she would ever return. She had just reached the street in front of the Pico Hotel and was looking up at Milagros's room. The window was dark. There was something terribly final in that black pane of glass.

She paced in front of the hotel for almost an hour, her thoughts lingering over this too brief reunion. They had hugged in the hallway outside Milagros's room, crying and laughing, and then her sister had pulled away and said, "Go, Izzie, before you're hurt."

Sister Ria had gazed into her sister's lovely face and whispered, "I present to you La Conquistadora, she fears nothing. *Ruegue para su alma.*"

The wind was blowing in from the high deserts to the north, blasting bits of dirt and dust over the roadway. Sister Ria was still standing in the street, reluctant to leave, looking up at Milagros's room, praying for her. Then she unfolded the piece of paper Milagros had given her and read the two names: L. Summerville and Samuel Atkins. They meant nothing to her.

The wind rose as Sister Ria crawled onto the buggy seat and started the little gray horse toward home. She watched the shadows along the empty street, remembering what Millie had said about the danger. The clop of the horse's hooves was comforting.

She stopped the carriage and looked back at the hotel. Milagros's room was still dark. "La Conquistadora," she whispered, "pray for her soul." But the words did not sound right spoken in English, so she said them again in Spanish: *"Ruegue para su alma."*

The buildings and sidewalks of the American part of town were empty of people and lit by lamplight. She glanced at the closest glass globe, watching its flame hissing in the night, the yellow glow ominous now. Down the street, she could see the dark roofline of the headquarters of the Los Angeles Gas Company.

Could Milagros be right?

"No," she whispered. Milagros just loved their father too much to be able to believe him guilty of murder, that was all.

Sister Ria was about to slap the reins on the rump of the little horse when she heard the sound. She sat up straighter. The wind was rising and falling as it shot through the gaps between the buildings, and she wasn't certain what she'd heard. Then it came again, shrill piping above the gusts. "Holy Sister." The voice of a child.

"Yes?"

Nothing.

"Hello?" she called.

Sister Ria reined the horse in a wide arc back toward the mouth of the alley where she thought she had heard the voice, guiding the animal into the narrow passageway as far as the faint slice of lamp-light, then halting. The walls of the buildings broke the force of the gale, but they also trapped the floating dirt, creating a thick fog of drifting silt in the dark passage.

"Child, where are you?"

Sister Ria squinted into the haze, searching for movement, a re-flection of light, anything that might be a lost or injured child. There was nothing.

She could hear water dripping.

"Say something."

Silence.

She waited until she was convinced she had been imagining things and began to back the little horse out of the alleyway.

"Holy Sister!"

The small voice leaped out of the wind and darkness at her. Sis-ter Ria jumped down from the carriage and moved toward the sound, her eyes sensing objects in the gloom more than actually see-ing them.

"Talk to me, child!"

She was deep in the alley, choking on dust and standing in a muddy pool of inch-deep water, peering into the darkness, her mind confused. The voice had sounded so close and desperate. Had she walked past the child in the darkness? She began to slowly retrace her steps, searching for an open pit or doorway where a child could hide. Nothing. Then she remembered Millie's warning and straightened up, sweat breaking over her skin.

If she wanted to be murdered, this was a good place. The buildings were windowless sheets of brick, the alley as lonely and dangerous as any she had ever seen in Poona or Calcutta. The walls and wind would smother any sounds of struggle. No one would hear.

She did not want to die.

She would find a policeman to search the alley with her. Slowly, she backed toward the carriage. The stench of raw sewage burned her eyes. "Child," she called one more time. She thought she heard voices in the darkness. But it was only the wind on brick. Was that all she had heard in the first place? She was no longer certain, and fear was growing inside her.

She was hurrying toward the carriage when she heard them again. The words were filled with panic: "Help me, Holy Sister!"

She turned back and ran, feeling down the brick wall with her hands, jumping over pools of water and piles of garbage, her body drenched in sweat. She had almost reached the end of the alley when she saw a broken place in the wall a few yards ahead, a dark entry, but not completely dark—a vague glow emanated from the tunnel-like passage.

She stopped. "I'm here, child—where are you?" She inched forward.

The narrow passageway reeked of urine. But it was empty. She waited, trembling and staring at the light beneath the door at the end of the tiny hallway. The wind had died momentarily, and she stood in the envelope of darkness and listened. Small sounds in the night became footsteps, the wind a hissing breath. Every fiber of her wanted to turn and run. But she had heard the child and would not leave.

"God give me strength," she whispered and pushed the door open.

The small storeroom was empty. There was an open doorway in front of her that led to another room. But her eyes were not on the second room; they were focused on the light that had drawn her here. Candles burned around a shoe box–sized nativity manger on the floor. The light cast a wavering glow over a tiny unborn lying in Christ's place. The child's eyes were dark holes, the body dried and mummylike. Without knowing how she knew, Sister Ria was certain this was Dorothy Regal's missing child. She could not look away from the empty eyes.

Fear was breaking over Sister Ria in waves when she heard the sound of someone running down the alley toward her. She spun around, her fists clenched, and looked into Clemente Rojo's face. From the direction of the second room, she heard something moving.

She started toward the sound, but Clemente held her back.

"You don't know who's in there," he said.

"A child is in there," she said, struggling.

"Listen to me."

She stopped.

"You stay," he said, pulling a small silver-plated pistol from his pocket. "Understand?"

Sister Ria nodded. The pistol had surprised her. "Please hurry."

Clemente moved past her and disappeared into the second room. She listened to him walking around, then moving heavy objects that sounded like boxes.

When he returned, the editor looked at her and shook his head. "Nobody—just an open window and an empty courtyard."

"No child?" she asked.

He shook his head again.

"We have to find it."

"I'll look again. You stay put." He studied her face to make certain she would.

She nodded.

Clemente went back into the second room, and Sister Ria listened; it sounded like he was going out a window. She knelt next to the tiny corpse, slowly rocking back and forth on her knees, her hands pressed together in prayer.

A large black moth was fluttering around the candle flames, the drafts of heat wafting the moth up and down over the fires until it banked away, circling and then landing on the shriveled face of the dead fetus, its wings opening and shutting slowly. Sister Ria drew in a sharp breath and wondered if the moth were the Antichrist in another form, come to claim the infant's soul. "Leave, in the name of Jesus Christ," she said. But it did not leave, and she struck at it, causing it to swirl in the backwash of her swing. It climbed the wall, batting its wings as it searched desperately for an escape. Exhausted, it landed on the dirty plaster.

Sister Ria stood slowly, her eyes locked on the dark creature. "Get out," she shrieked. "In the name of the Lord, get out!" She grabbed an old broom lying on the floor and smashed the insect against the wall.

She was on her knees and gazing at the dark smear of the moth's body when Clemente came back. He looked at the side of her face, then at her clenched hands. Her breath was coming in short gasps.

"Sister, are you all right?" he asked, leaning down and studying her features.

Sister Ria struggled to find her voice.

"Are you all right?" he said again.

She nodded and tried to stand, but her legs gave way. Clemente caught her. "The child?" she asked.

"I'll keep looking." Clemente gazed down at the manger. "Dead for some time," he said.

She didn't answer; her eyes were fixed on the moth.

He looked at her. "This isn't a good place at night."

While she liked the man, she wondered what he was doing here at this hour. "How did you find me?"

She thought he took too long to answer. "I was headed back to my office from the hotel when I heard you calling someone. You sounded frightened."

But the answer seemed right. She nodded and knelt and placed a handkerchief over the dead child, praying silently for a few minutes. When she stood, her legs were still shaky. She stumbled, and Clemente caught her shoulders again, steadying her until she was able to pick up the manger and the child.

Clemente reached for the manger. She hesitated and then handed it to him and started out the door.

That was when she saw it.

Someone was standing in the shadows a few yards down the darkened passage. She moved toward the shape.

Immediately, the figure started off at a loping run.

"Wait!" she yelled. But the person did not wait. The shadowy shape was moving fast, and Sister Ria was having a hard time following with her eyes.

"You wait!" she yelled again, then started after. The figure turned down a side passage. Seconds later, Sister Ria reached the same narrow lane. She slid to a stop.

There was a streetlamp at the far end that cast illumination down the passage's full length. She sucked in her breath. Nothing was moving. There were no doors, no windows, no side passages. And there was no one else. The surrounding walls rose fifty feet on either side, the narrow lane dead-ending into another wall. There was no one. She shuddered and stepped into the passageway.

Something moved. She squinted into the night, following a shadowy beastlike creature as it ran away into the darkness. She trotted after it, slowing to a walk as she neared the end of the passage. Whatever it was had stopped moving. She crept forward, her body shaking. Then she saw it and let her breath out.

"Sister, what are you doing?" Clemente called out to her.

"Nothing," she said, watching the frightened dog running away. She was still breathing hard when Clemente Rojo joined her.

"What's wrong?" he asked.

"Someone was standing in the alley watching us. You saw them."

"The dog?"

"No—a person."

Clemente studied her face. "No, Sister. I didn't."

She stared down the narrow lane again. "Well, someone was here."

"Where did they go?" Clemente asked, still watching her.

The growing frustration she had been feeling for days broke inside her. "I saw them!" she snapped.

"I'm sure you saw something, Sister." He paused. "There's a lot of dust."

"No, listen to me! I saw a person." She stopped talking and straightened her habit. Then she tipped her head at Clemente. "Forgive me. I'm sorry. There's not much light. Maybe I didn't see anyone." But Sister Ria knew what she had seen. She turned and started for the carriage at a fast walk. The young editor followed her.

Clemente placed the small manger and the infant on the carriage seat and took her elbow to help her crawl up. She was still shaking. The man stepped to the front of the horse and backed the animal out of the alley, studying her face. She knew he thought she was a lunatic, hearing voices, seeing people who disappeared, chasing after dogs. He probably thought she had placed the dead child in the room. She didn't care.

Clemente was standing in the street looking up at her. "You don't know who it was?" he asked over the howling wind.

He had clearly tried to sound as if he believed her. She was certain he did not. Her head was pounding. "No, I don't."

She was clucking the carriage horse into a walk, leaving Clemente behind in the center of the road, when she saw the small man in the brown suit and dark fedora. He was standing in the shadows on the other side of the street, smoking a cigarette and watching her. He was the same person she had seen in the marketplace that morning. Before she could see his face, he flicked the cigarette away and started off down the sidewalk toward the hotel. She slapped the reins on the rump of the little horse, steering the animal toward him. Perhaps he had seen the person going in or coming out of the alley.

"Excuse me, sir," she called.

The man did not stop walking.

"Sir?" she called again, louder.

But the man ignored her and turned in to the front door of the Pico Hotel. Surely he had heard her. She pulled the carriage to a stop and watched him disappear into the crowded lobby.

Clemente Rojo continued to stand in the middle of the road, watching her yelling at the man. Then he started off toward the offices of *La Verdad*. She slapped the reins on the rump of the horse and headed for home at a fast trot.

✝

The hacienda was dark. But Sister Ria needed no light to find the storage room. She was feeling with her hands across the top shelf, groping in the darkness. She struggled with a match and lit the candle in the wall sconce. She could see the darker rectangle in the paint where the nativity manger had sat for years on the shelf. It was gone.

She came out of the storage room, moving fast, and did not stop until she was standing in front of her father's bedroom door. She put her ear to the wood and listened. The room behind the door was silent. She knocked. There was no response. Suddenly angry, she wondered why she even bothered knocking and shoved down on the heavy bronze lever, pushing the door in. The room was every bit as dark as the hallway.

"Father."

Silence.

She moved past the tall candelabra, touching the candles. Cold. She yanked the curtains away from the wall. The sheets of his bed were cool to the touch, the top of the stone slab icy. She searched through the closets and the two armoires that held his costumes, looking for anything that would make some sense out of the confusion in her mind. Nothing. She wandered around in the shadows of his bedroom and began to cry.

When she stopped crying, she was standing in front of a curtain at the rear of the large room. She wiped her cheeks dry and pulled the cloth back and stood looking at a small door. She had seen it before over the years, but she had never seen it open nor known what was behind it. She knocked softly. No answer. She tried the handle: locked. She took matches from the side table and was starting to strike one when the bedroom filled with lamplight. Sister Ria turned and faced Aba. The old woman did not look pleased.

"May I help you?" Aba asked sternly.

"My father—where is he?"

"Obviously not in his room. And you should not be, either."

"What is behind this door, Aba?"

"Nothing that belongs to you, child."

Sister Ria wiped sweat from her face. "I need to know."

"Things of the patrón."

"What things?"

"Personal."

"Books?"

"I don't know what you mean."

"Are there books inside the room? Specifically, a book of Tennyson poems?"

Aba studied her face. "No."

Sister Ria leaned close to the door. "Father, if you are in there—"

"He is not."

"Then where, Aba?"

"I have no idea, child. It is not my business. Nor yours."

"The nativity manger is missing from the closet."

The old woman shrugged. "Many things are missing. *Los ladrones*—"

"I found it in town—there was a dead child in it—" Sister Ria stopped and caught her breath.

"And you blame your father for this?" The old woman paused, her eyes narrowing. "You told me you were going to try and save him."

"No, Aba. I said I would look into Dorothy Regal's death. That's all."

"You find these things, and you blame your father."

Sister Ria didn't know who to blame. But the blue manger belonged to the Lugo family. And if he had murdered Dorothy Regal and taken her unborn child, it would have been just like him to place the fetus in the alley as a mad joke. Yes, just like him.

Sister Ria lit a kerosene lamp and moved past Aba back out into the long hallway. She began a search of the house, room by room. Aba followed. They did not speak. When Sister Ria had searched every room and was convinced that her father was not inside the hacienda, she turned on the old woman. "Perhaps you believe you are helping him, but you are not."

"Isadora, your tone," Aba chided. She paused. "The patrón wanders the grounds at night. You are well aware of that. It helps him to think and then to sleep."

Sister Ria shook her head, then turned and walked quickly out the door.

"You must slow down, child."

Sister Ria whirled around. "Where is he?"

"Do not speak to me in that manner, Isadora."

Sister Ria trotted out into the darkness of the night. She

searched the gardens and work sheds, then moved quickly through the huge equestrian barn, the horses watching her. When she had not found her father, she headed back to the Lugo family chapel and the dead child she had placed on the altar.

Don Maximiato Rialto Lugo looked like a small boy playing at being a Catholic priest. He was standing before the altar in purple vestments, a white satin sash around his narrow waist, his arms thrown wide in an urgent appeal to the heavens. He turned and swung a filigreed silver ball on a long chain, dispensing clouds of sharp-smelling incense through the shadowy air. Candles burned on both sides of the altar.

Sister Ria stopped at the edge of the front pew and genuflected, doubts clouding her mind. She had not expected to find him here. If Aba was right—that he had simply been wandering the grounds— then Milagros could be right.

"Father, where have you been?"

He was speaking in broken Latin verses.

"Father?"

"Have you no respect?"

"You are not a priest."

"I can—" was all he said.

"Father, listen to me."

He was mumbling something.

"I will have a priest come in the morning for the child."

"No."

"Yes. The child must receive the holy sacraments and be buried with her mother." She watched him. He looked lost in deep thought. She cleared her throat and said, "Where were you tonight?"

He turned and looked down from the altar at her, intensely focused, like the white herons that stalked fish in the sea marshes. He was sweating in the cool air. Always he had been a difficult man—unstable, cross-grained, cynical, a scoffer—but now she sensed that he was truly insane. And if that was true, she could at least pity him.

"I have adventures with God," he said.

"Father, you are not well."

He waved her comment away with his hand. "I sleep in the arms of saints."

"You sleep in drugged stupors."

He tilted his head and appeared to be listening to a sound in the darkness that she could not hear, then he turned back to the altar. When he faced her again, he was holding the tiny corpse in his hands.

"Put the child down, Father."

He ignored her and stepped into the circle of candlelight, dipping a hand into the blessed water, dripping it over the shriveled body. "I baptize you in the name of the Father—"

Sister Ria was not hearing the words. She was staring at the bottom edge of his vestments, opening and shutting her mouth in small gasps. He was wearing riding boots and spurs beneath his robes. She jerked her head up, her eyes narrowing. "You were in that alley, in that room. You were there, weren't you?"

"—the Holy Ghost."

"Answer me!"

The cavernous equestrian barn was dimly lit by lanterns, the soft light wavering against the stone, reminding her of the convent. Sister Ria darted in and out of the stalls, startling horses as she went. Auel, the old barn master, trotted behind her, hat in hand, looking worried.

"I am not checking your work," she said, walking past the little man.

Six stalls later, she found what she was searching for. She yanked the blanket off the back of a sorrel mare, the little horse twitching and jittery, her eyes rolling to white at this woman in her black robes running a hand over the damp rectangular saddle mark on her back. Sister Ria gazed blindly at the stable wall. Finally, she said, "Who rode this animal tonight?"

"She is the patrón's."

Sister Ria had turned and was walking quickly toward the huge door of the barn when she saw a shadow on the wall stir. "Auel, who else is in here?"

"I allow no one in the barn at night."

"Father?" she called.

There was no response.

"No one, Señora."

She stood watching the shadows. "Yes, there was someone."

"Perhaps a possum. They hunt the young pigeons."

"No," she said, her eyes searching the darkness.

Auel took a lantern off the wall and turned the wick up, the flame rising and casting a wide circle of yellow light. He marched off down the hallway, hunting phantoms and muttering to himself. Sister Ria followed.

They found no one.

But she had seen the shadow move.

The patrón was no longer in the chapel. Sister Ria ran down the dark service road, through the courtyard, and into the rear of the hacienda, moving down the loggia toward his room. Her eyes were still adjusting to the deeper darkness inside the house when Aba loomed in the shadows in front of her, leaning with both hands on her cane.

"Why are you doing this, child?"

There was a chair next to the wall. The old woman had been waiting for her, Sister Ria realized. Her anger grew. "Where is he?"

"Dressing for bed. And you will not bother him."

"Yes, I shall bother him!" Sister Ria cried. "I did what I said I would: I looked into Dorothy Regal's murder . . . and I know now that he killed her. He is a murderer. Do you understand, Aba?"

"Do not speak such things."

"He murdered that girl and her unborn child." Sister Ria was rushing her words.

"I have asked you—"

"No, no, you can't protect him! He killed that—"

The slap was fast and hard, jerking Sister Ria's head to the side, silencing her as if the words had been knocked from her mouth. Slowly, she began to sob, her body heaving with each surge of breath.

When she was able to control herself, she wiped her eyes on the sleeve of her habit and looked at the servant. Aba was staring at the floor.

"Why have you stayed with him all these years? Why, Aba?"

"Forgive me, child. I had no right—"

"Why, Aba? Why have you stayed?"

The old woman just shook her head. "Forgive me."

"I forgive you. Now tell me why."

Aba turned and began walking down the hallway.

Sister Ria watched until she found her voice and said, "You love him."

Aba did not answer.

"Aba?"

The woman continued down the hall, disappearing into the shadows.

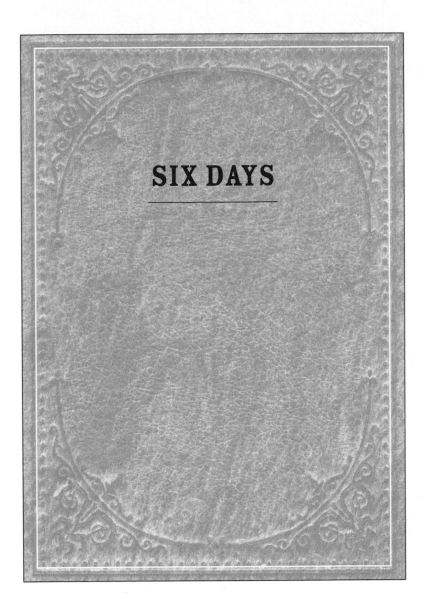

SIX DAYS

CHAPTER 10

THEY WERE LINED UP in the predawn darkness of the hacienda's loggia, just outside the patrón's bedroom. It looked like a police raid. Sister Ria had organized it as soon as Aba had left with Valla, the cook, for the morning shopping in the marketplace. The women would not be back for some three hours.

Min was standing at the head of the line, looking sick to his stomach. Sister Ria stepped up to him. "Key, please."

He looked even sicker.

"Min, give me the key."

The boy fished a ring of keys from his gown and reluctantly handed them over.

"Thank you," she said, knocking on the heavy door. When there was the usual silence, she said, "Father, we are coming in." She turned to the line of servants—Min and two other male servants and four cleaning maids—and said, "He will yell, he will threaten, but you must do as I instruct. Is that understood?"

They all looked pale, as if they had been given an order to stop a charge of Russian Cossacks with their mops and brooms. Several of them nodded nervously.

"Good. Pick up your equipment." She turned the key and shoved the door open.

It was the first time in her life that she had ever seen the patrón surprised. He was lying under his covers, glasses on his nose, propped up on pillows and sketching on a pad, smugly confident that his door was locked. His mouth dropped open.

For a long moment, no one said anything or moved. Then Don Maximiato yelled, "Aba!" as if he were being attacked by savages.

"She is at the market," Sister Ria said, waving the line of servants inside, "and we have come to clean your room."

"You will not!"

"You can stay in your bed, and we will clean around you. Or you can leave."

"You insolent child!" he shouted.

"It is for your own good. The room is filthy and not healthy," she explained, knowing that was not the reason. She had come to search for the book of poems. The day before, she had hurriedly looked for it while he was painting in the garden and had not found it. This time she would take the room apart shelf by shelf, drawer by drawer, cover by cover.

Don Maximiato had gone back to sketching, ignoring the servants while they stood staring at him, looking as if they were about to bolt.

Sister Ria ordered, "Take all of the animals out to the barn so they can be cared for properly. Then I want the flowers thrown away and any food removed to the kitchen for the cooks to look over." She was pacing back and forth through the maze of crates and baskets, as she had daily walked through the overcrowded wards of the lepers, giving instructions to the Indian orderlies. Fernando followed close behind her, looking as though he had assumed the role of second in command. "Then the closets and chests are to be emptied and the contents taken out on the veranda to air. Understood?"

No one moved; their eyes were locked on the old patrón.

"Is that understood?" She clapped her hands, and the spell was broken and the work began.

An hour later, the room was almost empty and Sister Ria was going through the drawers of a tall chest that stood across the room from her father's bed. They had not spoken during the entire procedure. The patrón had remained in bed, sketching madly and talking to himself.

He looked up at her and pulled off his glasses. "Do you find sin confusing?"

"No, Father, I don't."

"I think God got it backward. Sin is good; avoiding it is bad."

She ignored him.

"Making love, for example—"

She whirled and faced him. "Do not talk of such things in front of these young women."

"Is that a sin—to talk about making love? It isn't making hate."

She ignored him again and went back to searching the drawers.

"Do you dread hell?"

"Must you prattle on so?"

"Do you fear death?"

She was humming softly to herself.

"Do you take showers in your robe?"

She turned and looked down at him. "No, Father, I do not. Please get out of your bed so that we can change it."

"I've heard that."

"What, Father?"

"That nuns shower in their robes."

"That's ridiculous. Why would they do that?" she said testily.

"So God does not peek."

The servants giggled.

"That is enough. Get out of the bed."

"No—you get out of my room."

She pursed her lips. "If you do not get out of the bed, we will take it apart while you are still in it."

In response, the patrón disappeared beneath the covers, thrashing and scurrying about.

"What, pray tell, are you doing, Father?"

He mumbled something, but she could not make out the words. Moments later, his head popped out of the covers again. "There," he said, sounding smugly satisfied.

"There what, sir?"

"There, I am naked—so go ahead and take the covers off."

The servants froze.

"Entirely naked," he piped.

Sister Ria looked at him for a time and then said, "Rosita, María, Fabia, and Dolores, please leave the room."

"Totally, absolutely naked."

. . .

They had stripped the bed a quarter of an hour ago, and the pa-trón had been standing like a plucked chicken in a corner of the room ever since. Twice, Sister Ria had offered him a robe, but both times he had petulantly refused. She was watching Min and the other male servants turning the mattress. The book was not in the room. The only possible place left was the side room.

"Father, where is the key to the side room?"

As he had been doing periodically since he had been forced from the bed, he bent over and put his hands on his bony knees and aimed his posterior at Sister Ria. Min and the other male servants began to giggle.

"¡*Silencio!*" she snapped.

Her father straightened up.

"Thank you for your cooperation," she said. "I will find the key later. Min, please make up the patrón's bed before he catches pneumonia." Sister Ria turned and started for the door.

"Nun, I have a gift for you," her father said, tearing a page from his sketch pad.

She turned back and took the offered paper. It was a drawing of her, stark naked and taking a shower, a large crucifix dangling between her breasts. Through a nearby window peeked a bearded old man with leering eyes whom she knew could only be God.

Sister Ria tore the paper into small pieces and tossed them on the floor.

"I thought you had come to clean my room," he chirped.

CHAPTER 11

MIST FROM THE SEA was mixing with the morning sunlight, spreading a red hue over the walls of the hacienda's kitchen, when Sister Ria entered. She was exhausted, frustration building in her chest. They hadn't found the book, and she didn't know what to do. Aba had returned from the market an hour earlier and organized the reassembly of the patrón's bedroom. She looked up now as Sister Ria walked past, watching her as if she were a misbehaving child. Sister Ria avoided the woman's gaze and sat in a chair at the opposite end of the long kitchen table. Valla, the cook, and three other maids were preparing the noon meal, filling the large room with the sound of clanging pots and pans and idle chatter. Sister Ria took a steaming cup of Mexican coffee from a silver tray held by a young servant girl. "*Gracias,*" she said.

The girl curtsied and then stood looking at Sister Ria. She was perhaps fifteen or sixteen.

"What is your name, child?"

"Cristina, Señora," the girl said.

"It is nice to meet you, Cristina."

The girl looked anxious.

"Child?"

"May I speak with you?" Cristina whispered.

Aba looked up from her seat at the far end of the table. The old woman was sitting between two young maids who were busily cleaning the family silver. "Cristina," she said, her voice sharp. "You know better than to bother the señora."

"She isn't, Aba," Sister Ria said, and to Cristina, "Certainly."

The old woman ignored her and pointed at a broom leaning against a wall. The girl set down the silver tray and hurried over to it. "Perhaps not, but she will behave properly." The old servant's chin elevated slightly. "Contrary to what you may believe, Isadora, there are proper ways to behave in this life."

"The room needed cleaning." She put her hand inside her pocket and idly fingered the telegram that had come the night before.

Aba, ever mindful of her role as head servant, did not continue the discussion in front of the others. She looked instead to a small alcove at the far end of the kitchen and suddenly clapped her hands. "Work!" she snapped.

Sister Ria jumped. There were fifteen or sixteen children seated on reed mats around a small mountain of red peppers, sitting so quietly that she had not noticed them in the kitchen's bustling activities. Some were no older than five or six, their small hands running heavy needles and string through the pepper pods so they could be hung to dry like bright red and yellow necklaces on the adobe walls. The children were barefoot and in rags.

Sister Ria stood and walked over and smiled down at them. "*Buenos días, niños,*" she said.

They looked nervously at Aba.

"Street orphans," Aba said, "sullen. They come, they eat, they steal, and they leave. Sometimes five, sometimes twenty-five. They are a plague but the patrón still takes care of them."

"No. God's special children, Aba," Sister Ria said, smiling down at them. The children smiled back. She ruffled the hair on a skinny copper-headed girl of four or five. The child stood and raised her arms to Sister Ria. She reached down and picked the girl up and held her on her hip.

"The patrón feeds them," Aba said, "and fusses over them."

"They do not look fed, Aba."

"I make them work first." Aba stood up at the table's edge between the two young maids, watching as they polished the silverware.

"Please feed them now, Aba," Sister Ria said, her thoughts leaping to the orphan children of Poona. She held the little girl tighter. "What's your name?"

"Señorita Elosia Doloritas Concepción María Angel," she said proudly.

"Your mother gave you that name?"

"No. I made it up. Do you like it?"

"It's lovely. But it's awfully long. How about Angel María? Will that do? It's quite beautiful."

The girl grinned. "Yes. I like it."

"*Bueno.* That's what we will call you."

Aba was staring down silently at the tabletop.

Sister Ria looked back at her. "Aba?"

Aba did not respond.

Sister Ria looked at the children, her eyes locking on the oldest child among the orphans, an Indian girl of twelve or thirteen. She was tall and slender, with a beautiful face and sweet grace to her movements. But she was filthy and too far into her womanhood to be wearing paper-thin rags.

"Aba? Did you hear?"

The old servant looked up from the silver cleaning and watched Sister Ria for a moment before she called out in a husky voice, "Valla, prepare the meal for the strays."

"Thank you," Sister Ria said, "and in the future please call them children." She kissed the top of Angel María's head and then set her back down on the ground and returned to her coffee and the telegram. She read it again: *Santa Osita. See governor—two days. Nothing you can do. Leave. Millie.* Hope surged in her that Millie would be able to stay the madness. She mouthed a silent prayer for her sister.

Finished, Sister Ria sat half listening to the idle chatter of the servants as they went back to their work, the voices recalling to mind her sisters in India. She missed them. She even missed the never-ending litany of nursing and feeding, cleaning the great corridors and huge high rooms, scrubbing the stones, washing the filthy bedding and clothing of the sick and dying. Constantly exhausted by the drudgery, they were never able to quit because the tasks were never done. And God would never be satisfied until they were.

Sister Ria noticed the older Indian girl watching her. "Come here, child," she said.

The girl hesitated and looked at Aba.

"The doña has asked you to come, so go!" Aba said.

The girl jumped up as if shocked, and walked in a scuttling motion toward Sister Ria, dragging one of her feet as if it were a bag of sand.

Watching her move, Sister Ria realized the girl was even lovelier than she had first thought, even with the deformity. The child stopped in front of her, gazing awkwardly at the floor.

"What is your name?"

"Estrella, Sister," she said, still staring at the floor. "I'm sorry. I have never been here before. I was hungry. So I came."

"You are welcome here." Sister Ria smiled. "Look up at me, please."

Slowly, the girl raised her face.

Sister Ria examined her features carefully before she said, "Yes, I thought so. You are indeed one of God's stars in heaven."

The girl's face brightened some, but she did not smile.

"How old are you, Estrella?"

The girl was looking back down at her shoes. "I don't know, Sister."

The child's embarrassment reminded her of her own childhood. Sister Ria pressed her lips together against the sadness and turned to Aba. The old woman was growing increasingly unhappy with these unscheduled interruptions of the pepper stringing. "Aba, please have the maids prepare a bath in my room."

"Now? At midmorning?"

"Yes, please, now." To Estrella, she said, "Come with me. I'll have a meal brought to you."

Sister Ria was starting for the door when her father came marching into the kitchen, followed by Min and two young Mexican servants. All were carrying armfuls of brightly colored toy drums, horns, and whistles that they began to distribute to the laughing children. Don Maximiato was dressed in a bandleader's uniform, an ostrich plume stuck on top of his tall white hat. *He looks like an organ-grinder's monkey,* Sister Ria thought.

"Fall in!" he yelled.

Sister Ria watched him in disbelief. Six days from his own execution, and he was playing foolish games with children.

The children were banging and blowing on their new toys, the noise deafening. Aba looked angry—the patrón, gleeful.

"Don Maximiato," the old servant said over the din, "the pepper stringing."

"Fudge the pepper stringing. *¡La música!* Line up—line up!"

The children had obviously played this game before and quickly lined up in ranks of two, forming a long uneven queue in the kitchen.

"Father," Sister Ria said.

He did not respond but instead moved a sad-looking fat boy with a bad case of mange to the lofty position at the head of the line, patting the boy's shoulder. "Beat your drum loudly, Julio—we will march to the sound of it. Shoulders back, chin up." The boy looked proud.

"Father," she repeated. "The children have not eaten."

He held up his hand to the children. "*¡Atención, músicos!*" he shouted, and the noise stopped. "Do you want to eat or play?"

"Play!" the children screamed.

He turned and looked at Sister Ria. Then he looked at Estrella, seeming to notice her awkward stance, his eyes moving down to her misshapen foot.

Sister Ria tried to stop him. "Father, do not—"

He ignored her, pursing his lips as if in deep thought. "I have not seen you here before. You have a splayfoot—no, it is a clubfoot."

Sister Ria could see the embarrassment on the girl's face.

"Let me see it," he said, bending down and grasping the shoe and tugging it off.

"Father, please," Sister Ria whispered.

"Be quiet. It is not your foot." He stopped and looked up at Min. "Do we have enough instruments?" he asked, as if this were very important.

The boy nodded. Don Maximiato examined the misshapen foot.

"The children need to eat and they need shoes before they need toys," Sister Ria said. "Even you must—"

"Isadora," Aba said firmly.

Don Maximiato held up his hand again, this time to silence the old servant, his eyes on Sister Ria while he put the shoe back on Estrella's twisted foot. The children were standing at attention in their long line. For a brief moment, Sister Ria thought that her father might actually agree with her. Then Don Maximiato patted Estrella's shoe and let it go and filled his lungs with air and shouted, "*La música!*" and the children began to play a mad collection of discordant notes and banging sounds until she wanted to cover her ears. Sensing the line was about to move, Sister Ria grabbed a plate stacked high with freshly baked cookies and hurried to the kitchen door. "*La música!*" the patrón yelled again. Moments later, they were marching in ragged order, Don Maximiato high-stepping like the bandleader of an insane asylum, while Sister Ria passed out cookies at the door. Fernando, his tail stuck high in the air, followed smartly behind. Aba just shook her head.

Sister Ria was holding Angel María's hand and pacing her steps to the hobbling gait of Estrella, the three of them headed down the long hallway toward her bedroom when the young maid Cristina stepped out in front of them. "Good Sister," she whispered, her eyes darting nervously down the loggia toward the kitchen.

"Yes, Cristina?"

"Last night I heard you tell Señora Aba that the manger of Christ was missing." She gulped some air. "And that you had found a dead child in it."

"Yes?"

The girl hesitated.

"Go ahead, child. Nothing will happen to you."

"I saw the patrón walking with it near the work sheds."

"When?"

"After we had cleaned the blood from your room." The girl lowered her head, ashamed. "I was with the boy—"

Sister Ria looked at Angel. "Cover your ears."

Angel frowned. "I'm not dumb."

"Cover them anyway," Sister Ria said, turning back to Cristina. "Yes?"

"I was kissing my boyfriend when I heard someone outside and looked down and saw the patrón walking toward the work sheds, carrying the manger. It was very late—"

"Are you sure it was the patrón?"

Cristina nodded. "It was dark, but I could see. He was wearing his gaucho hat and a black cape that I have seen him in."

"Cristina," Aba snapped. The old woman was approaching down the hallway from the kitchen. "I have already told you once this morning not to bother the doña."

"Thank you, Aba, but it is I who bothered Cristina." Sister Ria turned and nodded at the young girl. "Thank you, Cristina. You may go about your work now."

"Yes," Aba said, "your work."

The girl hurried away.

In the distance, the children's mad music could be heard—something wildly joyous in the sound. But Sister Ria's thoughts were on the manger and the dead child and what Cristina had told her. Estrella had dried off from the bath and was behind the dressing screen, trying on clothes. Angel had fallen asleep on the bed. Aba stood by the door, looking as if she had fingers drumming inside her head.

"The dresses were purchased for you, by your mother," Aba said.

"And never worn."

"And should not be worn by—"

Sister Ria looked at her, and something in her eyes caused Aba to hesitate. When the woman continued, she said only "by anyone." She turned and searched through a small jewelry box on top of the chest of drawers, removing a garnet clasp.

"I wish to remind you," Aba continued, "that you are the daughter of the patrón. That you have responsibilities." She laid the garnet brooch and a black scarf on top of the chest.

Sister Ria watched her. "May I speak to you in the hall, Aba?"

The servant tipped her head slightly. "Of course."

Outside in the loggia, Sister Ria looked out the window at the morning mist burning off the distant fields. Aba stood behind her. Without turning, Sister Ria said, "He was seen carrying the manger from the house. The manger I found the dead child in, Aba."

"Is that something Cristina has said?"

"It doesn't matter who said it. He took the manger from the house, and I found the dead child in it."

"The girl is becoming bothersome."

"Listen to me, Aba. It doesn't matter who said it. It happened."

"I say the patrón did not do these things. I have told you that before."

Sister Ria turned and studied Aba's face for a long time before she nodded and started back into the bedroom.

Aba grabbed her arm and turned her around. "No, you will not walk away. I raised you, Isadora Victorine, and you will hear me out," Aba snapped. "You have stood against your father for too many years. He is going to be executed. It is time you put away what was done. If you don't, child, you will end up hating yourself for hating him."

"This has nothing to do with me."

Aba was trembling now. "Do not tell me a lie, Isadora!" she hissed, looking to see that none of the servants or the young girl in the bedroom were listening. "I will leave this house before I will allow that."

Sister Ria remained at the window for a long time, listening to the faint sound of the children's wild music. She could hear Aba talking in the bedroom behind her, the woman's tone once again that of the head servant. Sister Ria turned and walked back into the room. Angel was still asleep.

Aba nodded respectfully as she came through the door.

Estrella looked lovely in a simple yellow dress, standing and staring down at the cloth as though it might disappear if she looked away. "The hem must be lowered to a proper length," Aba said. She walked over to the chest of drawers, running her hands over the top. She turned and looked at Sister Ria. "I laid the scarf and brooch here—"

Sister Ria nodded.

"They are not here." The old woman turned to Estrella. "Did you take them?"

Estrella shook her head. "No, Señora. I would not have done such a thing."

"Of course you wouldn't," Sister Ria said. "It's probably one of the younger servants playing a joke."

"They do not do such things in this house, Señora," Aba said, still staring at Estrella. Estrella shook her head.

The door to the central garden was open, and Sister Ria stepped out into the sunshine. No one was there, and she returned to the bedroom. "Estrella, take off the dress so that it can be altered, and put on the blue one. It will do for now. Aba will find everyday things for you to wear."

Sister Ria waited until the girl had disappeared behind the screen before she turned to the old woman. "The brooch and scarf will show up."

"The girl is a thief."

"She is not a thief, Aba," Sister Ria whispered.

"Do you see them?"

Sister Ria glanced around the room. "They have been misplaced, that's all. But it doesn't matter, Aba."

The old woman stared at the tile floor, then looked up at Sister Ria. "They are your things, Isadora."

Sister Ria nodded. "Please have Min put a sleeping cot in this room for Estrella. She is too old to sleep unprotected at night. And please find work for her in the house." Sister Ria looked at Angel asleep on the bed. "Find a second cot for Angel. She is too young to sleep alone." Sister Ria thought a moment and then said, "I want all of the children housed either in the hacienda, the chapel, or the vacant servants' quarters."

"You are now the doña of the hacienda," Aba said, as if this would bring a halt to Sister Ria's madness.

"No. I am not the doña of this household. But I want this done."

The old woman gazed at Sister Ria, then tipped her head. "As you direct."

✝

Min had brought Sister Ria the news of the young messenger's arrival moments before, and he was bowing in front of her. She was carrying Angel on her hip.

"Min. Please." The teenage servant straightened and smiled and walked quickly down the hallway toward the messenger.

Sister Ria followed. The boy looked as if he had run all the way; his rough clothing was damp with sweat. Min inclined his head toward Sister Ria, and the young messenger trotted down the hallway toward her. As he approached, he took off his hat and stood with bowed head until Sister Ria stopped in front of him. Aba watched from an open doorway.

Sister Ria smiled. "Who are you?"

"Francisco, Sister. I have been sent by Monsignor Abel." He stopped and cleared his throat.

"It is a pleasure to meet you, Francisco," she said, setting Angel María down on the ground and pouring him a glass of water from a pewter pitcher on a nearby table.

He drank the water down without stopping. "*Gracias,* Sister." He panted, smiling. Then the smile left his face. "The monsignor wants you to know that he cannot do as you wish."

"Is the monsignor ill?" Sister Ria asked.

"Not when I left him, Sister—he was eating his breakfast and looked fine. He said only that your father had committed mortal sin and that the child and her mother also died in sin." Francisco had pulled himself up straight and stiffly delivered the message with the full force and gravity of his office as messenger for the Catholic prelate of Los Angeles.

Sister Ria bit at her lip and then turned to Aba. "Please see that Francisco has something to eat and then is driven back to town."

"*Gracias*," the boy said. "Do you have a message for the monsignor?"

Sister Ria shook her head.

Angel stuck her tongue out at the boy.

"Angel María, you stop that immediately," Sister Ria said.

"Then you have no message for the monsignor?" the boy asked again.

Aba turned her thin shoulders to the young messenger, her expression hawklike. "Yes. The Lugo family has a message for the grand personage. Tell him that we did not expect him to come—our invitation was merely a formality, a simple courtesy. Extended and now withdrawn. I will have it written out so that the monsignor receives it all. Every word." She looked at Min. He started to bow but caught himself and stood straight. Aba glared at him. He bowed. She nodded.

When Sister Ria next saw her father, he had abandoned his role as leader of the children's marching band and was dressed in the bright orange robes of a Tibetan monk, his head covered with a goatskin cap. She had sent Angel to play with the other children. Don Maximiato was standing in a large sandy circle behind the gardens, rocking back and forth on his spindly legs, crouched and high-stepping like a skinny sumo wrestler, holding a long hickory stave in his hands. A dozen Mexican workers lined the edge of the circle, while one of their own was dressed in an awkward-looking suit of padded straw, resembling a fat scarecrow. The man was wearing one of Don Maximiato's medieval jousting helmets and holding his own heavy hickory stick.

Twice the size of the patrón, the man was smiling confidently from behind his raised visor. Grunting loudly, he shoved his staff in front of him as if pushing back invisible opponents. The men standing around the circle were nodding and elbowing one another. The patrón ignored them all, still high-stepping, then slammed his long stick down on the earth as though he were killing snakes, chanting in a language Sister Ria had never heard before. Min was standing stiffly to one side of Don Maximiato, holding a large silver tray with a glass and a pitcher of water on it, a white towel over his arm. The boy bowed when he saw Sister Ria approaching.

"Stop that, Min," she snapped, her patience wearing thin.

The boy stood and grinned. There was a group of orphan boys standing behind the young servant, calling out encouragement to the patrón. Don Maximiato turned and waved at them and then went back to killing the invisible snakes. Time had mellowed him, but it had not mellowed her hatred of him.

Fernando was sitting at the side of the dirt circle, looking as if he were thoroughly enjoying himself. "Father, I need to talk with you," Sister Ria called from the edge of the circle. The workers were pulling off their hats and crossing themselves at the sight of her. She blessed them with the sign and then turned back to her father. As she did, the big man in the straw suit pulled off his heavy helmet and stood with his head respectfully bowed. "Bless you, sir, but I would defend myself at all times against this man," she said to him.

The caution came too late.

Her father had stopped high-stepping. He raised his staff over his head with both hands and yelled, "Eiieeee," then attacked the man, who was fortunate enough to get his helmet back on his head before the first blow struck. The man staggered forward and then began swinging wildly at the leaping figure of her father. The men and children were cheering. Fernando was clicking his teeth, his one eye glued on the battle.

Sister Ria shook her head and stomped back to the hacienda.

CHAPTER 12

EVEN IN THE SUMMER HEAT, her bare head felt cool without the veil, and she ran her hands repeatedly through her short hair, her mind churning the happenings of the past few days over and over. "I'm trying, Mother," Sister Ria mumbled.

Dr. Johnson cleared his throat. "Isadora?" He was writing at his desk, the listening tube hanging from his neck tapping quietly against the wood as he worked.

"Nothing, Doctor."

Tall, bald, and somewhere in his seventies, Reed Johnson had been the Lugo family physician all her life. His office was on the fourth floor of a building on Main Street, and across the boulevard, Sister Ria could see the headquarters of the Los Angeles Gas Company. She had checked, and the offices of Lawrence Summerville and Samuel Atkins were on the fifth floor. She knew she had to talk to them. But she had no idea how to do it. She couldn't just ask if they had murdered Dorothy Regal. She had no evidence. None. Only Milagros's suspicions.

Dr. Johnson turned on the stool and faced her. "You can get dressed now," he said, nodding toward the canvas screen in the corner of the room. "As a nurse, Isadora, you know the health laws that most countries follow regarding leprosy: You are to be quarantined for two years if you show any sign of it."

"Yes," she said from behind the screen.

"You could have hidden the fact of your exposure."

"No, I couldn't," she said. "I gave my word to the Indian officials that I would have an examination here in Los Angeles."

Johnson smiled as if she had said something humorous. "Then, of course, you had to do it." He smiled again and said, "I see no sign of the disease."

Moments later, she stepped into the office and adjusted her veil.

He studied her face. "How are you?"

She did not respond.

"You seem well."

Sister Ria walked to the window as if she had not heard. Johnson watched her for a moment and then said, "Close the door on the past, Isadora."

He continued talking sympathetically about her early years, but Sister Ria wasn't listening. She was listening instead to the echoes of her life in this place. At last she turned and faced him. "All I ever wanted was to mean something to him," she interrupted.

Johnson studied her face.

"I'm a nun, and I'm rotting inside with hatred."

"In his way, he—"

She held up her hands and shook her head. "Please don't. I don't want to hear about his so-called love. It never existed."

Neither of them spoke for a time. Sister Ria had moved back to the window. "There are children at the hacienda," she said softly.

Johnson looked up at her. "Yes?"

"They need to be examined by you."

"They have been."

"No. These are orphans."

"Yes, the orphans. Your father has me examine them twice a year. He's quite adamant about it."

✝

The tiny brown adobe was wedged between two towering brick buildings, a Mexican holdout against the Anglo sprawl of new Los Angeles. Sister Ria didn't know where else to go. She had prayed to God, but nothing had come to her. She was being led by a pretty girl of seventeen or eighteen through a small cottage garden filled with red and white hollyhocks and a patch of medicinal plants.

The girl, who called herself Ofelia, smiled at Sister Ria and knocked on the sagging wooden door of the primitive mud house. When there was no response, Ofelia, who had said she was the great-great-great-granddaughter of the curandera, Nachita, pushed open the door and motioned Sister Ria into the dark one-room adobe.

Sister Ria stood in the shadows of the ancient house, breathing in the smells of a hundred years of smoke and burning herbs and joss sticks, letting her eyes adjust to the darkness. The curandera was sitting in a worn armchair in a corner of the room. The fireplace was blazing, even though the morning air outside was close to ninety degrees. A thin sheen of sweat broke over Sister Ria.

"Grandmother is never warm these days," Ofelia said, removing the shawl from her shoulders. "Is that not right, Abuela?"

The old woman stirred like a hibernating animal. Sister Ria's eyes had dilated to the point where she could see the shrunken figure clearly—her shoulders draped with a heavy black shawl, a dark bandanna tied over her head of thin, wispy white hair. She had a shaking palsy in her right hand. Her face looked like a dried apple core, the eyes lost in slits of sagging skin.

"How old is Abuela?" Sister Ria asked the girl.

"One hundred and fifty years," Ofelia said proudly.

That is impossible, Sister Ria told herself.

"What have you to ask of my grandmother?" the girl said.

"A woman was murdered two months ago, not far from this house. Her name was Dorothy Regal. Abuela, did you know her?"

The old woman neither moved nor spoke.

"Grandmother charges a fee for her services."

Sister Ria placed a gold coin on the table next to the old woman.

"I knew no Dorothy Regal," the old woman wheezed. "I knew a whore."

"Yes, that was her."

The old woman shrugged. "If you say."

"Did she come to see you?" Sister Ria asked.

The old woman nodded.

———

"What did she want from you, Abuela?"

"To be out of danger."

"What danger?"

The old woman appeared to drift off into slumber. The granddaughter looked at Sister Ria and said, "The woman was afraid."

"Of?"

"Someone had been following her. She was afraid of what they were going to do to her."

"Did she say who was following her?"

The old woman was snoring softly. Ofelia shook her head. "No. Just that she was being watched, and she wanted Abuela to prepare a potion to protect her."

"It did not save her," Sister Ria murmured.

"Abuela did not prepare it. The woman would not pay."

"I found a piece of paper in her room with the words *Brown cutaway.*"

The girl nodded. "Yes, I remember. That is what Abuela told her that she read in the smoke."

"What does it mean?" Sister Ria asked.

"Abuela?" Ofelia said.

The old woman tipped her head toward the girl. "What do the words *brown cutaway* mean? You told the whore those words," Ofelia said.

The old woman sat for a time and then just shrugged.

"She often doesn't know the meaning of what she reads in the smoke," Ofelia explained.

Sister Ria pulled herself to her full height. "I have a question, Abuela."

"You want her to read the smoke?" the girl said.

"Whatever she does, yes."

"There is a separate charge for this reading."

Sister Ria placed another coin on the table. Ofelia scooped some coals from the burning fireplace with a small iron shovel and poured them into a heavy metal crock in the center of the table. Then she helped the old woman pull her chair close and guided her gnarled hands into the rising columns of smoke. Sister Ria's eyes burned.

"What do you ask her?" the girl said.

Sister Ria hesitated, then cleared the smoke from her throat and said in a quiet voice, "Did my father murder Dorothy Regal?"

Ofelia did not appear startled by the question, and Sister Ria guessed that the young girl had heard hundreds of ugly secrets in this dark room.

They waited. The old woman said nothing, her eyes closed. Ofelia whispered something into her ear, but she just sat, her withered hands blackening slowly in the smoke. Then Nachita shook her head.

"I'm sorry. Abuela sees nothing," Ofelia said.

Sister Ria was turning to leave when the old woman began to flex her fingers in the rising wisps, grasping at the strands of gray vapor. "The boy," she murmured.

"The child in the alley?"

The old woman shrugged.

"I don't understand."

Nachita shook her head, annoyed by the distraction, and again milked the smoke with her hands. Then she took a sudden deep breath and bitterly spat out, "Dragged to death." She opened her eyes and looked at Sister Ria. *"No accidente."*

Sister Ria brought her hands to her face, palms pressed together, her thoughts flying backward in time to the summer of her sixteenth year.

She had hidden in her bedroom the evening he came calling. Ruperto Tristan was from Mexico City, seventeen years old, worldly and handsome. He was spending the summer with his aunt's family, the Valdezes, wealthy Los Angeles merchants, and he had taken to Isadora as if her masculine clothing only enhanced her charms. While her father continued to demand that she keep her head shaved, she no longer wore the cascara. But even her tan skin failed to dissuade Ruperto.

Unlike Milagros and the other well-bred girls of the pueblo, Isadora was not chaperoned but, rather, left to do as she wished, and she and Ruperto had spoken many times on the streets. Once they had even walked boldly through the plaza gardens together, holding hands, her young heart speeding with joy.

Still, the night he came calling, she had panicked and hidden in her room. Young men came courting Milagros all the time. But none had ever come to see her. They were forbidden by their families to have anything to do with her—this half-man-half-girl who worked in the fields and barns in the company of the men of La Cienega.

So she had hidden. Hidden until Milagros found her and dragged her into her older sister's bedroom and forced her to put on one of Mil-

lie's lovely dresses. Then Milagros had wrapped her shaved head with a
beautiful blue silk scarf, pinning it, turbanlike, with silver clasps. Ruperto had never seen her without her hat. Isadora had made certain of
that. Milagros and Juanita and Carla the maids put a very fine and expensive cascara thinly on her cheeks and coloring on her lips, then pearl
earrings and a diamond necklace that had been their mother's.

As they worked over her, Milagros kept whispering into Isadora's
ear, "Do not let this boy go. You may not get another chance. Take this
one and get out of here."

Finished, Milagros dragged her in front of a long mirror. Isadora
was stunned. She felt beautiful. She had never felt that way before. She
never would again. The four of them held hands and danced and
laughed in a circle.

Aba had kept Ruperto occupied on the veranda, plying him with
sweet drinks on the hot summer evening. Don Maximiato had retired
to his room early, as he did each night.

Milagros shoved Isadora out the door of the hacienda toward
where Ruperto sat sipping a drink, watched over by Aba. Then the
two women withdrew, leaving Isadora alone with him. While awkward, it was not as difficult as she had dreaded. Ruperto was funny and
lively, and they were soon laughing and talking. Ruperto told her stories of the great city of Mexico, of his family, of trips he had taken. And
Isadora listened. Listened and felt like a young woman. It was a wonderful feeling.

Then suddenly, the patrón was standing before them in his nightshirt, holding a pistol in one hand and a fencing saber in the other.

Blue veins pulsed at the side of his head, and he was weaving in one of his drugged stupors. He said nothing, just pointed the cocked pistol at the chest of Ruperto.

Then Aba and Milagros were there, Aba talking the patrón down in firm but soothing tones, Milagros standing bravely between their father's pistol and the boy. The patrón raised the saber as if he might strike Milagros with it and instead poked it over her shoulder and deftly lifted the blue silk turban from Isadora's head, exposing her bare skull before he turned and walked back into the hacienda.

Two days later, a body was found on a lonely road south of Los Angeles. It had been dragged for miles behind a horse. Ruperto Tristan was identified by what was left of his clothes.

"Did my father murder Ruperto Tristan?"

The old woman shrugged. "*Accidente*, no," she repeated.

"Dorothy Regal? Did he murder her?"

The abuela grasped at the rising smoke, probing with her fingers in the drifting fumes. Then she dropped her hands in her lap and sagged back in her chair.

"Abuela?" Ofelia whispered.

The old woman cleared her throat and looked at Sister Ria and said, "*Cuidado*." Be careful.

Sister Ria walked slowly down the street away from the curandera's house, thinking the agonizing thought that, years ago, Milagros and she could have stopped this madness—could have saved Dorothy Regal and her baby. If only they had acted.

If only they had done what was right. Guilt flooded over her as she recalled the night a few months after Ruperto's death.

Isadora had slept in the barn most of that week, working alongside the herders as they tended the birthing ewes. It was early evening, and she had just come inside the hacienda for an extra blanket and stopped by Millie's room to say hello.

Millie was sitting on her bed, staring down at something in her palm.

"Millie?"

Milagros jumped and closed her hand over the piece of gold. But Isadora had seen it. It was a man's ring: a golden eagle's head. Ruperto Tristan's ring.

"Where did you get that?" Isadora demanded.

Millie wrapped the ring in a lace handkerchief and then looked up at her sister. "If I tell you, you have to promise to never say anything."

"Millie, that's Ruperto's ring. Tell me!"

"Are you sure it was his?"

"Yes, I'm sure. Now tell me."

Millie shook her head. "Not until you promise you'll say nothing about it."

Isadora pressed her lips together and nodded.

"No, say it: 'I promise.'"

"I promise."

Millie got up and shut the door to her room. "You really promise?"

"Yes, I promise! Now, where did you get it?"

Milagros studied her sister's face and then said, "Father's room. I was looking for a piece of Mother's jewelry and saw it. I wasn't certain that it was Ruperto's, but it looked like the ring he was wearing the night he came to see you."

Isadora put a hand to her mouth and closed her eyes and slowly shook her head. "Father killed him."

Millie grabbed her by the shoulders. "Stop it. We don't know that. He could have found it on the road where they found Ruperto. Or Ruperto could have lost it here at the house that night. Maybe the ring was too big for him. Maybe one of the servants found it and brought it to Father."

"Or maybe he took it from Ruperto's finger," Isadora moaned.

"Izzie, don't talk like that."

"What are we going to do?"

"Nothing."

"Nothing?"

"That's right, nothing. Izzie, listen to me. Ruperto's family is very powerful. And Father is known to be argumentative."

"Mad, you mean."

"Stop it, Izzie. If we tell anyone that we found Ruperto's ring in Father's room"—Millie stopped and looked into her sister's face—"if we tell, we will have sent him to be hanged."

Isadora sat and thought before she asked, "Then what are we going to do?"

Millie lowered her voice. "We are going to get rid of it."

Isadora swallowed hard and nodded.

They melted the ring in the forge behind the barn. And Isadora kept her promise.

Sister Ria shuddered hard at the memory and started walking again. She had to know the truth now. This was no longer something she was doing for Aba. She had to know for herself. She had to know if she could have saved the woman and her child.

✝

The place felt different in broad daylight—muddy and smelling of garbage but no longer frightening. Sister Ria, bent at the waist, slowly retraced her steps down the alley, studying the sticky earth beneath her shoes. Clemente Rojo was struggling with a heavy tripod and camera. She waited for him to catch up.

Sister Ria had not found what she was hunting when she pushed open the door to the small storeroom and stood looking down at the melted candles on the floor. She glanced up at the white plaster wall and froze. The dark smudge of the moth's body was gone; the wall showed no sign that the creature had ever been smashed against it. She shuddered and crossed herself. Frantically, she hunted for the broom. It wasn't there, either.

Clemente watched her. "Do you want to leave?" he asked, his voice concerned.

She didn't answer.

He bent in front of her and waved his hand. "Sister, are you in there?"

"Yes, I'm sorry."

"Do you want to go back?"

"No," she mumbled, her heart pumping hard.

"Sister, are you sure you're all right?"

"There was a moth—"

Clemente watched her face.

"I smashed it against that wall." She turned and looked at him. When he didn't respond, she said, "You saw it?"

Clemente shook his head. When he saw the fright in her eyes, he added, "But I wasn't looking for a moth."

"Well, it was there. I killed it."

Clemente's eyes searched the plaster.

"I killed it," she whispered.

✝

"There," she said.

Clemente set his large mahogany camera on its tripod in the back room, then squatted beside her and stared at the jumble of muddy footprints tracked inside from the alley. "Those are mine," he said.

"Are you sure?"

He stood and placed his boot in the print: a perfect match. "This is the print we want," he continued.

She studied the smaller boot print that Clemente was pointing at and nodded. She continued searching over the collection of footprints. "None here," she whispered.

"Sister?"

"There was no child here."

"It doesn't look like it."

The thought that someone had lured her into this place by mimicking a child's voice caused the hair on the back of her neck to rise.

Clemente was watching her face and looking concerned again. He patted her arm in a comforting way.

"I'm fine," she said.

He nodded, placed a ruler alongside the boot print, brought his camera over, and began to work with a series of brass screws until the lens was aiming straight down at the floor.

†

Sister Ria caught a small red horse-drawn streetcar at the corner of Spring and Sixth and rode it to Figueroa Street, where she got off and walked west down the tree-lined boulevard. The wide street was bordered by the oldest and most expensive Mexican homes in Los Angeles. She was thinking about her father—who he was or was not—and growing more and more confused as she turned up the brick path to her godfather's house.

Don José Vargas's elegant home was surrounded by a thick twelve-foot-high wall that protected it from intruders and road dust. One of his servants met her at the front door and led her through a heavy gate into a tree- and flower-filled courtyard alive with the sounds of parrots and fountains. It was also alive with the memories of her youth. The lovely grounds looked like early colonial Mexico. She had always loved it here. It had been her refuge in the pueblo—a place where she was accepted and loved; a place where she could escape her father.

They were walking deep in the garden when Sister Ria saw two peones squatting in a large dirt circle, shoving fierce-looking fighting cocks—necks extended, hackles flared—at each other. She had seen the rite hundreds of times and hated it.

"Do not let them fight," she said. The words echoed in her thoughts, releasing fragments of a dark past that instantly crowded in on her. The heat, the sleepless nights, and now the dark recollection caused her to stumble on the pathway. The servant caught her and guided her to an iron bench under a sprawling oak that she had climbed a thousand times.

"I'll get you some ice water, Señora," the servant said, hurrying away.

The two peones had turned and were staring at her, holding the birds suspended in the air.

"Do not let them fight," she repeated, the words themselves dragging the old memory back into her thoughts. She closed her eyes.

She was snaking cattle out of the hills with the vaqueros of La Cienega when they jumped him. They had been looking for him for weeks, had seen his kills on the grassy edges of the plains.

Felipe Bacus had dismounted and was hunting strays in a narrow arroyo when he stumbled on to him. The beast's right foreleg was broken. Even so, he was quick, and he caught the screaming Bacus in the dense brush.

Isadora reached them first, lunging her large sorrel gelding, Bisonte—the bison—straight into the giant bear. Isadora had always resisted riding the horse, but her father demanded it. Bisonte was the horse her father had ordered the barn master Auel to put into Garrapata's stall that morning two years before. She had always believed that he simply meant to further humiliate her by forcing her to ride an animal that looked like a gigantic plow horse. But in this frightening moment, she was thankful the huge horse was under her. Though terrified, he rammed the roaring bear, driving hard with his hoofs in an effort to roll the enormous brute.

The first charge did not stop the bear from mauling Bacus, and she backed Bisonte up for a second run. Isadora could hear the vaqueros urging their mounts up the narrow arroyo behind her, yelling at her to get away. But she would not. While she detested the role, she had replaced her dead brother as the patroncito of La Cienega. It was her responsibility. And she would not run from it.

Bacus was screaming when she put her spurs to Bisonte. Amazingly quick for his size, the horse slammed his great bulk into the bear, knocking it momentarily off the man and giving Bacus the chance to scramble for his life. Then the others were around her, yelling and throwing their ropes on the roaring beast.

Six riders held the lunging bear tethered between their horses by long ropes, hauling him slowly across the plain, the animal charging first one way and then another only to be pulled back by the strangling ropes. They dragged him, half choked to death, to the barricaded bull pen behind the horse barn. The patrón and the vaqueros stood on the wooden rampart, staring down at the emaciated beast.

"He's crippled," Isadora said.

"He tried to kill Bacus," the patrón snapped.

"Bacus surprised him."

She watched the herders driving one of the giant range bulls into a chute that opened into the pen. A heavy planked door blocked the bull's entry into the enclosure. "Do not let them fight," she said. The bull had smelled its old adversary and was lunging at the thick oak walls of the narrow passage.

The patrón looked at her. Then he yelled, "Open the gate!"

The bull took the bear from the side with a powerful lunge, goring the beast deep in its shoulder and driving him roaring into the wall of the pen. The grizzly was no coward and fought back, but the giant bull was too powerful, and the bear too weakened by starvation.

The bloody contest had been raging for some ten minutes, the men drinking hot beer and toasting the combatants, when the explosion shattered the afternoon air. The bear went down without a twitch. The men turned and stared in silence as Isadora leaned the rifle against the rampart wall, climbed down the ladder, and began to walk back to the hacienda.

In the stillness, the patrón began to slowly clap.

She shoved her thoughts back to the garden. The two peones had gone back to stabbing the birds at each other. "Did you not hear?" she asked in Spanish.

Through a nicely trimmed privet hedge, the voice of Don Vargas interrupted her. "Adolfo, please do as our good sister requests."

Sister Ria peered around the side of the hedge. Perhaps to remind himself of his poor pueblo roots, her godfather, José Vargas, was sitting in an old rocking chair under a roughly constructed Indian jacal of upright cottonwood poles and lighter crossbeams of ash. The three-sided structure was covered with grapevines. The old man looked weak, not as she remembered him. He was gaunt, and his brown eyes were sunk deep in their sockets, but he was still handsome, soft-voiced, and silver-haired. He bowed his head toward her and crossed himself with a heavy-boned hand; a guitar and blanket lay on his thin legs.

"Thank you, Don José," she said, smiling warmly. "I do not like to see them fight."

"Isadora, anything."

She stood and studied this old man she loved so dearly, noting his lack of surprise at her return to the pueblo after eleven years. Nor did he seem at all surprised that she had come back as a nun, as if he already knew. She smiled, certain he did. Don José was her godfather but he was also Los Angeles' only Mexican attorney and he had always amazed her with the little things he knew of the people of Los Angeles and the daily happenings in the pueblo—minute strands of detail woven into evidence, intelligence, and explanations. And she had come to him for just that reason: to unravel the knots of questions inside her head.

He had represented her father during the murder trial and lost, but still, he might have the answers she needed. "It is wonderful to see you, Don José. You look well," she lied.

"Old," he said, "but you, sister of the Virgin, are young and very beautiful." He waved a hand. "Come sit and talk with me. Pretty girls rarely do anymore."

Sister Ria laughed and walked over and kissed his cheek. Don

José was not only her father's attorney, he and her father were also old friends. Twice he had served as *alcalde*—mayor of the pueblo of Los Angeles. But that had been a long time ago.

"It is wonderful to see you," she said again, putting a hand warmly to his cheek.

"And you, godchild," he said, struggling to his feet and setting aside the guitar and blanket. He grasped both of Sister Ria's hands. She could feel a tremor in his arms. Then he sat back down as if the effort were too much, still smiling at her. He took in the wimple, the stark white scapular, the shapeless cloth.

"I had heard of this," he said, making a proud sweeping gesture at her robes with a large liver-spotted hand. "Most lovely of nuns, Sister Ria—I believe."

"Yes." She laughed. He even knew her name.

"Sister Ria. Wonderful."

She glanced at the exquisite garden and the magnificent house. "Successful as always, Don José."

"Only modestly able to survive." The teasing sound left his voice. "How is the patrón?"

Sister Ria just nodded.

The old man studied her face and started to say something, then seemed to change his mind and let her little act of rudeness pass unchallenged.

They sat in the shade of the jacal and laughed and chatted about times past, and she relaxed for the first time since she had come back. Listening to Don Vargas's voice, she remembered why she had always loved him. He had been what her father had not: interested in her and caring. The servants brought steaming cups of dark café and small rich sugar cakes. Sister Ria balanced the cup and a cloth napkin on her thigh for a while before she set it on a side table and looked at the old man, her expression serious. "The men at the gas company—"

"How is Milagros?"

"Fine. She'll see the American governor, asking for a postponement of the execution." She paused and studied the old man's face. "Will he grant it?"

Vargas looked down at his hands for a time, staring at them as if they belonged to someone else. Finally, he glanced up at her and shook his head. "It is hard to say. He refused when I asked him several weeks ago. But Milagros can be very convincing. Let us hope."

"Do you believe what she believes?"

"About Summerville and Atkins?"

"Yes."

"No. I do not. I had men I trust look into it. They found nothing. It is true they tried to buy La Brea. They made offers, through me, many times. But that doesn't make them murderers." The old man took a sip of coffee, his hand dwarfing the small cup, then set it on the table and sat watching the steam rising from the dark liquid. "Milagros does not agree."

She rubbed her forehead with the tips of her fingers.

"Why have you come back, Sister Ria?" he asked.

"I promised Mother I would take care of him." She paused. "It was a childish promise."

The old man shook his head. "No. I think you came back for another reason."

"And what is that?"

"Your heart—it would not let you do otherwise."

"No, just the promise."

"Is it one you wish to keep?"

"I have no choice."

"We always have choices, godchild."

She pressed her lips together to smile at the old man. "And I have made mine."

They sat without speaking for a time, the way they had sat here so many afternoons when she was a child. At last, Sister Ria cleared her throat and, as if she were speaking to herself, said, "He never loved me." She stared at the earth between her shoes. "Dr. Johnson tried to tell me that he did. But he didn't." Her voice trailed off.

Vargas studied the side of her face beneath the veil, then he turned and gazed out across the garden at a pair of red-and-green Mexican parrots. The birds were screeching loudly in the hot afternoon air. "Ferdinand and Isabella are happy to see you."

She nodded and then stared back down at the dirt. "He never did," she said again.

Don José looked back at her. "You never really knew him."

"I knew more than I wanted."

Don José shook his head. "No. You knew the man he became after your mother died."

Sister Ria ignored the comment.

"He once dreamed of being a great artist," Don José said, as if he had been asked a question. "He was considered very promising in that world—so promising that he had been apprenticed by Johan

Jongkind, the great Dutch painter. As you know, Maximiato and I grew up together, were close as brothers. And I knew how thrilled he was by the chance to work under a master like Jongkind.

"All he wanted was to paint the sunsets of Sevilla—the Lugos' ancestral home." Don José continued to watch the parrots.

Sister Ria said nothing.

Don José cleared his throat and said, "Your grandfather Raúl was dying, and the Lugo family fortunes had shifted badly. Maximiato was told he must take over the affairs of La Cienega." Don José folded his large hands in his lap and looked at her. "And so he gave up his dream. Like mist in sunlight, it disappeared. He was no more suited to the life he was forced into than the little girl Isadora was." He reached over and fondly patted her hand. "Still, he did it."

Sister Ria pulled at the cloth of her habit. Finally, she looked up at him and said, "He was not the only one who had a dream."

"You never told me yours, dear child."

She shook her head. "It doesn't matter." In her entire life, she had told only Aba. But not even Aba knew how the dream still tugged at her. She shook her head again. "It doesn't matter."

"It matters, godchild." Don José took a sip of coffee. "Perhaps someday you will tell it to me. I would like to hear it." The old man closed his eyes for a few moments. When he opened them, he asked, "What was I saying?"

"You were talking about the running of La Cienega."

"Thank you. Ramón seemed so well suited to the task—as if he had been born to it."

"And then they were gone," she whispered.

"Yes. I believe Maxie could have survived the death of poor Ramón. But not," Don José said, shaking his head, "the loss of your dear mother."

"And I replaced Ramón."

"There was no one else."

"Milagros."

Don José smiled. "Milagros would not have done it."

Sister Ria looked down at her hands. "He had no right."

"Without your mother, something broke down in his mind."

They sat without saying anything for a time. Don José appeared to have gone to sleep in the sunlight. Then he stirred and said, "So he turned to you."

"You make it sound as if it was an act of love."

"No. An act of respect."

She blew air out her nostrils and said, "Respect was never anything he gave me."

"Respect that, young as you were, you could run the family's last holding."

"He was wrong," she said.

The old man's eyes met hers. "He has aged. We all have aged. Minds change." He gazed out at his garden as if he had finished, then took a deep breath. "But not hearts. Don Maximiato did not kill that woman. But I cannot prove it." He drifted off again.

A male servant in white came and touched him on the arm. "Don José, it is past your rest time."

"He was my friend, and I let him down," Vargas mumbled.

———

"I know you, Don José Vargas. You did all you could," Sister Ria said.

He sat up straighter, holding on to the servant's hand, and looked at Sister Ria. "Maxie should have taken it."

"Don José?"

"The few acres they wanted are worthless. He has little left."

"He has thirty-seven thousand acres."

The old man shook his head. "Most of it is gone." He picked up his cup and drained the last of the coffee, his hand shaking, and handed the cup to the servant. "American taxes." The sun was no longer on Vargas's face, and he scooted his chair to catch it, the way she had seen lizards move to the sunlight to drive the chill out of their bodies.

The servant stood by patiently, gently resting a hand on the old man's shoulder. "Then the Anglo squatters came and challenged the legitimacy of the title grants, and the ranchos were forced to prove ownership." Don José shook his head, blue veins pulsing at his temples. "It is an impossible task—the grants are a hundred years old, vague boundaries. Your father had me fight them for years. I hired Anglo lawyers who knew the American laws. All of that cost large amounts of money."

"How much is left?"

"Of La Cienega?"

"Yes."

"Perhaps one thousand acres. No more."

She drew in a sharp breath.

The old man's eyes were shut again, his face turned up to the sun. She waited for him to look at her. When he did not, she said, "I found a book of Tennyson's poems in Dorothy Regal's room."

"The patrón did not kill the woman."

"And a piece of paper with the words *curandera* and *brown cutaway* written on it. Did any of those things come up during the trial?"

He shook his head.

"Do you know what they might mean?"

"No. I do not. I know only that the patrón is not a murderer."

Sister Ria's thoughts leaped to the night she and Millie had melted the ring in the forge. Reflexively, she started to say something, then remembered her promise and said only "There were questions about Ruperto Tristan's death."

Vargas patted the servant's hand, indicating he would like to get to his feet. "He is not a murderer." He looked at Sister Ria. "I am old now, you must excuse me. It is good for these eyes of mine to see your lovely face." He gazed at her. "Do you remember what I used to call you?"

She nodded. "*La niña testaruda.*"

He smiled. "*Sí,* the stubborn child," he said, reaching out and playfully tugging her nose. "You should not be stubborn any longer." He watched her face for a time before he said, "Forgive him—for your own sake."

She said nothing.

"Be proud of him."

She shook her head.

Don José settled back into the chair as if her refusal had further

weakened him. "Godchild," he said, sounding exasperated, "your father is a great man." He gazed through the vines at the blue sky
above, seemingly searching through his memories.

The servant grasped Don José under the arm, but he shook his
head. "When we were young, Sister Ria, he and I went out with
General Pico to fight the Yankees the day they came to take our
pueblo and our land. We met them in Cahuenga Pass. There were
hundreds of them and only forty or fifty of us." Don Vargas began to
chuckle. "And General Pico determined in all his soldiering wisdom
that a hasty retreat was strategically wise for our cause." The old man
smirked. "I agreed wholeheartedly." He paused and caught his
breath. "But not your father."

Don Vargas pulled himself up straighter in the chair, his face
turning somber. "He flew into one of his furies—ranting and raging,
exhorting us to battle. But we were not convinced, and after a frus-
trating time spent challenging us to do our duty, he marched off to
his tent." The old man looked at her. "We all thought he was done.
But you know him, Sister Ria."

She pursed her lips and nodded.

"Minutes later, Don Maximiato came clanging back, dressed in
the ancient battle armor of a proud lancer of the conquistadores,
yelling, 'Who will join me in ridding our land of these *perros?*'" Don
José was chuckling softly again. "I will say that he looked very im-
pressive. But I am ashamed to add that none of us agreed to join him
in ridding the land of the Yankee dogs.

"He screamed, 'Hoist me onto my horse!'" The look on the old
man's face had turned grave.

"Don José," she whispered, "you need to rest."

"No. I need to tell you about your father. None of us would help him on to his horse. Then he looked at me and said, 'José, you must.' I remember to this day the look in his eyes. It made me proud to be his friend." Don José wiped his mouth with his napkin. " 'You will be killed,' I told him. 'Yes,' he said, 'but our honor will live.' " Don José dabbed at his eyes, overcome with emotion. "And so I helped him onto his horse.

"I was frightened and ashamed, and your father saw that. He said, 'It is all right, Joséy—I fight this day for us both because even though I know you would, you must not . . . you must care for my wife and guide my son in protecting the Lugo family.' Then he spurred his horse up and down in front of us, yelling, 'You have one last chance to join me!' When no one stepped forward, he trotted his horse out across the plain, his lance under his arm, calling in a loud voice, 'For the king of Spain and honor!' "

The old man stopped talking and gazed at the ground as if he could still see Don Maximiato trotting forward between the two opposing armies. "None of us thought he would actually do it—we thought he was full of foolish bravado and would soon whirl his mount and return to us, satisfied that he had faced the enemy. But he did not. One moment he had stopped and was sitting silently on his grand stallion—our own David facing Goliath—then the next, he was spurring his mount across the wide space, leaning forward with almost perfect lancer form." The old man was breathing hard, sweat breaking on his brow. "The Americans were laughing at him. They, too, expected him to turn and flee back to us. We stood dumbstruck by his courage. And then they began to fire.

"We could hear the bullets striking his armor. His horse staggered and almost went down from the withering fire, but Don Maximiato spurred him to his feet, and together they continued their mad charge. The Americans were no longer laughing."

"He survived," she said, determined to strip him of any glory.

Don José nodded. "Yes. How, I do not know."

The old man was shaking his head, lost in the back eddies of his mind. "We were certain he was dead. Fearing that his bold act of bravery would trigger a charge from the Americans, we turned and were quickly leaving the field, sadly defeated without firing a shot, when a cheer went up. We turned back and saw the patrón break free of the American lines and gallop back out onto the plain and stop. He and his horse—both of them gravely wounded—were about to collapse. Everyone on both sides just stood and stared in silent, almost reverent disbelief at this small brave man, who had become a giant to us on the Mexican side."

Don José looked at Sister Ria. "None of us said anything. I could not look at my friend. His courage had shamed me. Then I heard a man next to me whisper, '*Madre de Díos*,' and I looked up to see the patrón spurring his wounded stallion back into the American lines. We watched them both go down."

"He survived."

"With God's grace. He had been shot seven times—but he survived."

Sister Ria helped the servant lift Don Vargas from his chair. The old man stood watching her, worn down by the telling of the story. He said, "Forgive him before his death." He patted the servant's arm, and they turned and started toward the rear of the house.

"Don José," she said, watching Vargas and the servant. "I love you," she called.

They stopped, and the old man stood looking at her. Then he smiled and waved. The servant began to lead him down the path again. Sister Ria was standing and watching them and straightening her habit when she felt it: the piece of paper that Milagros had given her.

She had nowhere else to go.

CHAPTER 13

"MR. SUMMERVILLE will see you now."

Sister Ria followed the young American secretary, whose brass desk plate identified her as Marjorie, into a room that looked more like a parlor than an office. There were rich leather sofas and nice wing chairs, and the walls were paneled in dark oak with paintings of English hunt scenes. Was this the office of Dorothy Regal's murderer, as Milagros believed?

Sister Ria had no idea.

"Please be seated," Marjorie told her. The girl, maybe eighteen or nineteen, was grinning and bouncy and chewing on the end of a pencil. She eyed Sister Ria as if she'd never seen a Catholic nun before. "What's it like?" she whispered.

"Pardon?"

"Do you pray all day?"

Sister Ria focused on her. "No. Not in the Benedictine Order."

Marjorie chewed on the pencil a little more and then asked, "So what do you do?"

"I work with dying lepers."

The expression on the young woman's face transformed, as if she had just been shown her own death mask. She backed out the door.

"Thank you," Sister Ria called. But Marjorie was gone. Sister Ria sat down in a chair in front of an elegant old burl desk and forced herself to think about why she had come to this office. She waited a few seconds, then stood and hurriedly searched through the book-shelves behind the desk for the book of Tennyson. Not there. Quickly, she turned around and pulled open each desk drawer and peeked inside. Not there, either. Ashamed of herself for prying through another's belongings like a common thief, she returned to the chair and anxiously awaited the man's arrival.

Almost immediately, the door opened.

Sister Ria was not certain what she had expected Lawrence Summerville to look like, but when she looked up at him, she real-ized she had expected him to look different than he did. He was small, with bright red hair, a wiry build, and a priestly smile.

"*Bonos dyas,*" he said, cheerfully mangling the Spanish. Slowly, in English, he asked, "How is your English?"

She smiled. "Better than your Spanish."

He laughed. "Good. Then we can talk in English. I have been warned that you have leprosy. You're holding up quite well."

"I work in a hospital with lepers. I don't have the disease."

He looked serious. "It must be very sad work."

She nodded. "At times very sad."

Summerville picked up a thin black cigar. "Do you mind?" he asked, holding it.

"Not at all."

He struck a match, smiled again, lit the cigar, and said, "It is good to finally meet you." His voice was sincere.

Sister Ria took a deep breath and then said, "Don José Vargas doesn't think you would murder." She watched his face for a reaction.

He smiled. "You don't waste a lot of time warming up to things."

"I don't have much time."

"I understand," he said. "We didn't frame your father, like your sister believes."

"Or murder Dorothy Regal?"

"Of course not," he said, his voice rising slightly. "Our crime, Sister, was trying to buy a few acres from your father." He licked his lips. "These new electric companies are driving the price of street lighting down to where we can't continue to ship coal from Australia." He studied her across his desk. "We are going bankrupt, Sister."

She didn't say anything.

"We offered far more for the land than it could possibly be worth."

She stiffened. "And what exactly is my family's heritage worth on your American market?"

Summerville put his cigar in an ashtray and made a steeple of his fingers, looking over them and seemingly reappraising her, as if he had not expected anything but kindness and prayers from a sister of the veil. Then he turned his head and yelled, "Sam!"

The side door opened, and a thin bespectacled man with a fringe of grayish hair stepped into the room. "Larry?" This man looked even less dangerous than Lawrence Summerville.

"Sam, this is the younger daughter of Max Lugo."

She did not care for this Anglicized version of her father's name. "Don Maximiato Lugo, the patrón of La Cienega," she said stiffly.

"Yes, I'm sorry," Summerville said, looking, she thought, more annoyed than apologetic. "Don Maximiato." He glanced at his partner. "What was the amount we offered for the acreage?"

"Seventy-five," Samuel Atkins said, his voice a high-pitched falsetto.

"Seventy-five thousand, Sister. For seventy-five thousand dollars, I should be able to buy the entire thousand acres of your father's land. That's a fair price for five acres, isn't it?"

She raised herself up slowly from the chair, her eyes fixed on Samuel Atkins.

"Everything all right, Sister?" Summerville asked, his voice less friendly than before. He watched her as if she might be daft.

She didn't care. Atkins's voice had sounded childlike, and she could not stop thinking of the small voice calling to her from the darkness of the alley. She was also remembering Milagros's certainty that these men had framed Don Maximiato for the murder of Dorothy Regal.

"Sister?" Summerville said.

She stared at the two men. "Do either of you read poetry?" It was a goad rather than a question.

"No," Summerville said. Atkins shook his head.

"Then you wouldn't have a book of Tennyson?"

Summerville watched her for a moment and then said, "Is that what you were rifling through my desk for?"

Her muscles tightened. He had been watching her, somehow, as she searched his office. "Yes," she said and walked out.

Sister Ria paced back and forth in front of the gas company office, rethinking everything Summerville and Atkins had said. It was evening when she stopped and shook her head in frustration. None of it helped her. The street was busy with wagons and carriages; she was standing and staring blankly at them when the young secretary Marjorie hurried nervously by on the sidewalk. Sister Ria felt bad that she had frightened the poor girl. Marjorie's sweetness and innocence reminded her of poor Elsie. Sister Ria leaned against the side of a brick building and shut her eyes and thought back to that horrible night.

The marriage had been arranged.

The terms set by Elsie Cordova's family and representatives of Don Maximiato Lugo. Money had exchanged hands and the agreement sealed. There was only one condition: The marriage could not take place before Elsie's fifteenth birthday. She had just turned fourteen when she arrived at La Cienega from her family's home in Barcelona. So Aba had set up a strict system of watchful sheltering to protect the honor of the girl, as well as the honor of the patrón. Don Maximiato had turned sixty that year.

The week before her death, Elsie had slipped into Isadora's room late at night and knelt by her bed and, whispering as if to hide from God, told her she was going to break her marriage promise, a promise made before God. "Will I be damned?" she had asked, trembling and grasping Isadora's hands as if they might keep her from falling into the pit of hell.

Isadora had taken Elsie into her arms. "Of course not—God understands."

The night it happened, Aba had been sitting in Elsie's room while Millie read the Bible to her, as their father insisted she do every night. Millie hated the task but did it, as she did all things he asked of her—with a sense of resignation and quiet dignity. Isadora could hear her sister's voice through the thick wall of her room. Then there had been silence. Millie had come into Isadora's room, rolled her eyes and shaken her head, and whispered, "My babysitting chores are over for the night," then kissed her sister good night and gone off to bed. Not long afterward, Isadora had heard her father—as she often did—humming Schubert's Impromptu Op. 90, No. 2, the only music he seemed to know. He was walking away from Elsie's bedroom, down the long hallway toward his own room.

The tapping sound began a few minutes later and drew her to the wall that separated her room from Elsie's, the sound like a soft hammering against the stone blocks. Isadora had stood waiting for it to stop. When it did not, when the slow, incessant rhythmic sound had begun to frighten her, she had broken Aba's rule and taken a candle and gone into Elsie's room.

The girl was hanging from the rafters—her face a horrid purple color, hell's light in her eyes—her foot still jerking reflexively against the wall.

In all the years since, Isadora had never understood why.

The three of them had planned out in detail Elsie's escape. It was to take place in only two weeks. Isadora had pilfered traveling money from the patrón's bedroom. And Millie had purchased the ticket that would get her on board a transport in San Pedro harbor that would take her to Guadalajara. From there she would travel by stage to Mexico City and refuge in the home of her mother's sister. All of this had been done in secret, and Elsie had appeared so thankful.

Why?

Nor was that the only thing Isadora questioned. The only piece of furniture in the room close enough and tall enough to stand on while Elsie drew the noose around her neck was a small stool. Yet it stood upright near the door, five feet behind her body.

Since then, Sister Ria had seen one other hanging. It was at the convent. One of the novices had taken her life. The poor girl had stood on a chair beneath the rope, then kicked the chair out from under her.

It made no sense.

Sister Ria was moving slowly, etherized by her worries. She wandered aimlessly up and down Main Street for the next hour, searching for what to do next. Then she gave up and turned down a side alley, headed back to her carriage.

In the shadows between the buildings, she could see someone standing next to her carriage. The person's back was to her. Her heart was pounding. "May I help you?"

The man in the brown suit started and ran down the narrow passage back toward Main Street. She followed, running hard as well.

Sister Ria was moving fast when she came out onto the wide

boulevard, crowded with wagons and pedestrians. She stopped and turned in a quick circle, looking for the little man. He was nowhere to be seen.

Who was he? To judge from his size, the man could have been her father or Atkins. But it had been dark between the buildings, and she hadn't seen him all that well. Suddenly, her thoughts were on her carriage. She whirled and trotted back.

Trembling, she stepped forward until she could make out the objects lying on the carriage seat. She clamped down on the air in her windpipe: There lay the garnet brooch and the black scarf that had been taken from her bedroom. And propped against the backrest of the carriage seat was the small wooden cross that had been cut from her cincture. The little man in the brown suit had sent her a warning. He had been inside the hacienda. So close to her that he had been able to cut her cross from her person. And if she didn't stop—he would come again.

CHAPTER 14

THE RIDE FROM TOWN seemed endless. Sister Ria tried to keep her mind from running off in a hundred different directions. But it was useless. At least one thing was absolutely clear to her: The man in the brown suit was not playing games. He was deadly serious. Again she told herself it had been her father. She frowned. It could just as easily have been Samuel Atkins. Or someone else.

She was still worrying the questions over and over in her mind when she drove the carriage through the open doors of La Cienega's large stone stables. Auel came out of his tiny office and took the reins.

"I hope you had a good drive, Sister," he said, yanking his straw hat from his head, "and that the animal behaved to your liking."

"Yes, Auel, thank you. The horse handled well."

"I am pleased."

She climbed down and watched as the old man unhitched the horse. "The patrón is called Santo," she said.

"*Sí.*" He nodded.

"*¿Por qué?*"

The old man looked at her and smiled. He was missing a front tooth. "Because he is truly sainted."

"I don't understand, Auel."

"He has given us a church, he doctors our sick, and now he cares for our orphans."

"The old plaza church, is it not yours?"

The old man shook his head. "It belongs to the Anglos. They pay American dollars for seats, Señora. We cannot. And the priests are Francos or Italianos."

"But it is still your church."

He shook his head again. "The mass is spoken in *inglés.*"

"It is still your church," she insisted.

"They do not want us there. We are nothing to them." He smiled at her. "But the patrón, he provides for us. He made bigger the Lugo chapel, and he marries us and baptizes our young, buries our dead."

"He is not a priest," she said softly.

"No, he is a saint. That is far better." The old man pulled the bridle off the little horse and turned and looked at her. "When the Mission San Fernando was open, the priests brought a doctor every month. But now the mission is closed, and there is no doctor. So the patrón has become one himself." The old man pointed at his missing tooth. "He pulled this for me." He smiled again. "He cures us like a worker of miracles. It is truly amazing, good Sister. You would be very proud of him."

She turned and picked up a large envelope lying on the carriage seat that Clemente had given to her that afternoon. She held it in her arms and watched the old man put a blanket on the sweating horse. Then she started for the door. "Thank you, Auel."

She would not debate canon law with the old man.

Night was thickening inside the great house. Sister Ria stood in her father's room, catching her breath and holding Clemente Rojo's package. She felt terribly anxious, as if her soul were about to dissolve.

No matter what she thought about her father, the fact that he was to be executed in a few days was a frightening reality that caused her to hurt somewhere deep inside. Her thoughts were jumbled again, and she struggled to stay focused. She had dedicated her entire being to things of the spirit, but now she was being undone by her human frailties.

"Mother, help me," she whispered.

Trembling, she unwrapped the package, laid it on the floor in front of the French armoire, and opened the beautiful walnut doors. She removed one of the patrón's tall riding boots, the same ones he had been wearing under his religious vestments in the chapel the night before.

Estrella had followed her into the room and was standing behind her, dressed in a bone-white servant's dress, her hair pulled up into a neat bun high on her head. Aba had done what Sister Ria had asked.

"Would you have me polish the patrón's boots?" Estrella asked.

"No, Estrella. You must go. Aba would not want you in my father's room."

The girl curtsied and walked to the door, then stopped. "Thank you, blessed Sister," she said. "For everything. You are as blessed as the patrón."

"I am not blessed, Estrella. Neither is the patrón."

"*Sí*—you are both blessed," the girl insisted.

"It is God who is blessed," Sister Ria said. "Now go."

Sister Ria sank to her knees beside the package, holding the boot in her hands, then placed the sole down on top of Clemente's large photograph of the muddy footprint in the alley. The ruler was lying next to the boot print in the picture. Clemente had used it as a guide to enlarge the photograph to exact scale. The edges in the mud were blurred, and it was not a perfect match—close but not perfect. She tried another boot with the same result: She wasn't certain. Still, it was close. And it was the only thing that made sense. He was the only person who knew the gardens and the house well enough to have stolen into her room in broad daylight and taken the brooch and scarf without being stopped. And only he could have crept down the hallway and cut her crucifix from her. For the same reason, he was the only one who could have killed the rooster in her room and then slipped out into the gardens and back into the house. Also, the young maid Cristina had seen him with the manger.

Sister Ria searched the closet for the brown jacket. Nothing. She sat down hard in a nearby chair. Estrella watched her from the open doorway, a look of concern growing on her young face. Unable to restrain herself, Estrella poured a glass of water and took it to Sister Ria, who drank it.

"Thank you, Estrella, but you must leave. You must not be found in this room." Sister Ria looked into the girl's face. "You must be careful in this house."

The young girl helped her up from the chair. "I don't understand, blessed Sister."

"You must always lock the doors—both the hall and garden doors—to my room when you sleep. Do you hear? And you must go nowhere alone with the patrón. Nowhere. That is a rule you must never forget. Do you understand?"

The girl looked frightened.

"Tell me that you understand, child," Sister Ria said, grasping Estrella's hands.

The girl nodded, her eyes wide.

✝

Later that evening, Sister Ria found herself in her mother's room, deep-cutting emotions weakening her. Opening the door to her mother's closet, she could still smell it: the wonderful faint scent of her mother's perfumes and bath powders drifting among the clothing. Kneeling on the floor, Sister Ria clutched in desperation at a dress hanging in front of her. "There is nothing I can do for him. Nothing!" Her voice turned into a moan.

She stood up slowly. "I can't save him." She buried her face in the cloth.

Some three hours later, Sister Ria was sitting in the library, working at the long table under the light of a single candle, trying to chart all that had happened over the past few days—all that she knew about Dorothy Regal's murder. Angel María was sitting at the far end of the table drawing on a piece of paper. Fernando hopped up onto the table and sat down near Sister Ria and watched her. "How have you been?" she asked the old cat. He stood and walked to the far end of the table and sat again, this time next to Angel. The old tom leaned forward and studied the girl's drawing like an art critic and Angel reached a hand out and scratched his ears.

Sister Ria straightened up on her seat, her eyes wide. "María, take your hand away from him," she whispered.

"Why?"

"He's not friendly."

"That's silly," María said, "we're friends." She pulled the old cat into her and rubbed her head against his.

"How do you do that?"

"Do what?"

"Get him to let you touch him."

María frowned at her. "I told you. We're friends."

Sister Ria stood and walked down to María and the old cat. María had drawn a picture of the hacienda, with stick figures standing on the veranda. The largest had a cross hanging around her neck and Sister Ria figured that one was her.

"Do you like it?" María asked.

"Yes, it's very nice."

Fernando stood and looked at the picture again, trying to figure out, she guessed, what all the fuss was about. Sister Ria slowly reached a hand out and touched the back of his head. And he bit her.

María was giggling and Sister Ria was sucking on the bite when Estrella walked into the room. "There you are, María," the girl said. "I've been looking for you. It's time for bed." Estrella had taken over María's care like a big sister.

"Yes," Sister Ria said, still sucking on her hand, "time for bed."

After the girls had left, Sister Ria returned to her chair and papers at the far end of the table. Fernando sat at the opposite end watching her. "I'm the one who rescued you," she said. Fernando stood and then sat again, his back to her this time. She ignored the cat and focused on the papers before her.

She had little more than a jumble of confusing facts and suspicions. Sister Ria shook her head and started writing again, then stopped and listened. Someone was talking and she was certain it wasn't Estrella and María. The noise was faint, but she could hear it. She got up and walked into the hallway, turning toward the kitchen. The sound was growing louder. She heard Aba's voice. The woman sounded angry.

"Aba?" Sister Ria said, walking into the darkened kitchen. It was empty, but the back door was open, and she could see the glow of lanterns in the small square where the large earthen *hornos*—ovens— were located. She stepped outside.

Aba was standing with her arms crossed over her thin chest. The young maid Cristina was in front of the old servant, holding a large butcher knife and looking frightened.

"I can't do it!" Cristina moaned.

"You will do it."

"Aba?" Sister Ria asked.

The old woman neither turned nor answered her. But Cristina whirled toward Sister Ria and moaned, "I can't do it—please don't make me, Señora!"

"Cristina," Aba snapped, "I have told you before that you are not to bother the doña. I will not tell you again."

"Aba?"

"I am simply doing my job, Señora, directing the servants."

"I am sure you are. And what are you directing Cristina to do?"

Aba did not answer, but Sister Ria could see that her body had stiffened at the interference. She was not used to having her directions to the servants questioned.

"Aba?"

"Give me the knife," Aba said sternly to the sobbing girl, "give it to me now."

The woman took the knife and walked over to the far wall of the enclosure. Sister Ria squinted into the shadows. Four large brown hens were hanging by their feet, tied to the wall with cords. Aba grabbed the head of the first bird and pulled its neck until Sister Ria thought the head must surely pop off; the bird's body was stiff, its wings spread out. With a quick slice of the knife blade, Aba decapitated the hen. The bird fell back against the wall, wings flapping hard, blood spurting. Aba stepped quickly to the second bird. "I have directed Cristina to prepare the birds for tomorrow's meals," she snapped, cutting the head off the second bird with the same efficient slice of the knife. "It is to be part of her job in the future."

The girl had turned away from the slaughter and looked ready to faint.

The four hens were beating out the last of their lives against the wall when Sister Ria said, "I am sure there is other work that is more suitable for Cristina." She could not take her eyes off the dying hens and the sprays of blood, recalling the rooster that had been killed in her bedroom. "I am certain there is other work for Cristina," she repeated.

Aba did not turn to face Sister Ria. "It is the job of the head servant to assign work, Señora."

"I understand. And I am sure you agree that Cristina is not suited for this work. Please find something else for her to do, Aba."

The old woman did not respond.

"Aba?"

The woman tipped her head stiffly. "As you direct, Señora."

"Thank you," Sister Ria said, turning to look at the young servant, who was sobbing without sound. "Cristina, please go to your quarters. Aba will have something for you in the morning."

Sister Ria waited until Cristina was gone. Then she looked at the old woman, who still stood with her back to her. "Aba, I want Cristina assigned to normal house chores. Do you understand? She is not to be punished for having spoken to me."

Aba said nothing.

Sister Ria walked back inside.

✝

Later that same night, the metal-capped heels of Sister Ria's heavy convent shoes on the loggia tile reverberated like castanets through the silence of the great hallway. The rooms were quiet, the servants off for the night. She walked slowly toward the only other sound: the faint chanting of a Buddhist mantra in the central courtyard.

Sister Ria stepped out into the garden. The chanting had stopped. Oriental prayer chimes gave off a soft shimmering sound in the warm night air. She saw him through a screen of ivy under the light of two lanterns hung on iron tripods, painting at his easel. He was dressed in the brown cloak of a monk, the cowl up over his head, his waist girded with a rough hemp rope.

"Father?" She could see his brushstrokes rapidly creating a rose in the shadowy light, the strokes almost furious. The painted blossom looked a living thing, and her mind jumped to thoughts of her sister, Milagros, and their childhood game. "Pray for her soul," she whispered. Sister Ria moved closer, her eyes focused on the cowl. The material blurred before her eyes, worry and lack of sleep overwhelming her. She forced herself to concentrate. "How are you, Father?"

"Do you know that you will find Pythagoras's theory of divisions in the work of all the great masters? Botticelli, Rembrandt, Vermeer—"

"I don't want to talk about that. I want to talk about you."

"No." He was hurriedly mixing rose madder, rose dore, and alizarin red, creating a vivid pink on his palette.

She watched him for a time before she said, "You need to confess the truth, Father."

He dabbed his brush in the paint.

"I know what you have done," she said. "I found the manger and the poor infant. I know about Ruperto Tristan. I know you have been following me. I know all these things."

She waited. Still he did not respond, and she reached and took the brush from his hand. "If you are trying to hurt me—" She stopped and looked at the side of his face.

He took another brush from the jar and continued applying paint to the canvas.

"This is about you, Father—your soul. You have very little time left. Tell God what you have done." She took a deep breath.

He continued working.

"Is this the way you would have it? Can you not sense the danger? You are sensing hell," she whispered.

"I am working!" he snapped.

"You have murdered three human beings," she pleaded. "You may not even know what you have done. You are ill, Father." She chewed on her lower lip until she tasted blood and then turned back to the hacienda.

She froze.

Aba was standing a few feet away in the shadows. The old servant glared at her through the darkness. "He did not do these things!" she snapped, turning and marching back into the house. Don Maximiato chuckled.

Sister Ria waited until Aba was gone. Then she looked back at her father. "Tell me that you killed Dorothy Regal!"

The patrón pulled the cowl off his head and looked at her and raised his eyebrows. "Calm yourself, child—wrath is the devil's web."

He had shaved his head and was bleeding in places from the razor, looking like some martyred saint. But he was no saint in her eyes. "Where is your holy priest?" he mocked.

Sister Ria had turned back to the darkened house when she saw Aba looking down at her from an upstairs window. She stood staring up at the old woman's dark shape. There was something unnerving in the silhouette.

"Your priest?" Don Maximiato asked again.

Sister Ria turned back to her father. "This isn't about priests. And if you won't let it be about your soul, then it's about nothing."

He grinned at her. "You had responsibilities—" His voice broke into a smoker's hacking cough.

"Yes," she said, jamming the brush back into the jar on his easel, splashing paint thinner on him. "To God," she hissed. She picked up a rag near his chair and wiped her hands clean.

He had returned to his painting and was quietly humming the same tune that she had heard him hum a thousand times. She felt the muscles across her shoulders tensing. It was the same tune she had heard him humming the night she'd found Elsie.

Sister Ria continued to watch him, her hands twisting the rag. She was shaking—growing increasingly frightened by her inability to stop fragments of the past from flooding in on her, mixing with the present like flood silt from a river. Her mind seemed determined to scourge these sharp remembrances for all time, to drag her hatred of him into the harsh light of consciousness.

Like Elsie, she had been promised in marriage. The memory danced before her.

She was sitting in the library, staring at the blackened wall of fire bricks lining the massive walk-in fireplace, and trying to remember her dead mother's face in the shadows, her head pounding. Her father was marching back and forth in front of her, dressed in a Mexican cavalry officer's uniform, with riding pants and knee-high boots and small silver spurs.

He stopped pacing and looked at her. "You will do as I have said."

It was close to midnight, and candlelight danced slowly on the walls.

"I will not," she said.

Don Maximiato started pacing again, like an actor on a stage. "I would not have decided this had it not been for your foolishness."

"Marrying God is not foolishness, Father."

"Do not say that again!" he yelled. Then he walked on and composed himself. "You will marry Don Lorenzo Cortés. It has been arranged. There are—"

"No, Father," she interrupted. "I am not Elsie."

"You will marry—"

"Do not risk your reputation on it," she interrupted.

"He is waiting in your room—go to him."

She laughed.

"You will be cared for," he continued. "La Cienega will be cared for."

Isadora's eyes were locked on her father's face, and she was nodding in a nonsensical way, as if agreeing with his every word. She looked away to the dying fire. Her head was hurting, and she massaged her temples with the tips of her fingers. "I am done here, Father."

"You will not leave until I say you can. You will not turn your back on your responsibilities. Do you understand?"

She continued to watch the embers of the fire, crying softly.

"Don Lorenzo will make a decent husband. Go to him."

"I am done, Father."

"You will stay with him this night!"

"This is not the breeding of cattle, Father. Such things are not to be done without sanctification of the church and God."

"You will—or I will dismiss the old woman!"

Instinctively, he had found the one place in her heart not hardened by callousness. Aba had become a mother to her. He knew that.

Isadora Victorine Lugo was gone the next morning.

But she would always remember that night . . .

Now the patrón looked up from his easel, his eyes mocking her. "You're shaking, child. Surely you're not afraid of your own father?"

"I shake for your sins," she said, starting back to the house.

"Nun," he called after her.

She turned back. "Yes?"

"It belongs to me," he said, pointing at the rag.

She sailed it into the night sky.

✝

It was late, and Sister Ria lay in her bed listening to the wind in the garden, determined not to think about the past. The room felt cold, and she rolled onto her side and pulled the covers up to her neck. Earlier she had heard Min and her father carrying the large easel down the hallway toward his bedroom.

The house was quiet now.

Sister Ria was dozing when someone tried the handle on the garden door. She bolted upright and held her breath and watched as the person tried a second time, the heavy brass bar lowering slowly. Then he or she pressed against the thick wood. The lock held.

Moments later, she saw a shadow at the shutters and heard pressure being applied to them as well. Also locked. She slipped quietly out of bed and moved to the door and peeked out through a thin gap into the night. Nothing. Fear grabbed at her like a hand from out of the dark, and she pressed against the wall and waited. The wind stirred the bushes outside her room.

Whoever the intruder was, he or she was waiting as well. There was no way they could know for certain whether Sister Ria was asleep or awake. As if her thoughts had reached the person, there came a soft knock on the garden door. She pressed harder against the wall, afraid to speak.

A voice, rushed and frightened, said, "Let me in. Please."

Sister Ria started to take a step forward, then stopped. The voice could belong to Cristina or Estrella or one of the other servants. Had her father tried to harm another woman? The words sounded badly strained, but so had the voice in the alley. Her heart sped. She waited, flattened against the wall.

The voice came muffled through the thick wood again. "Sister Ria. Please let me in." She could hear sobbing.

The desperate pleading tugged at something deep inside of her, and she moved quickly to the door before she realized it was locked. "Wait while I find the key." She stepped to the nightstand, her mind racing. Estrella was on kitchen duty and she kept Angel María with her. Sister Ria felt over the top of her nightstand for the key, picked it up, and hurried back.

"Estrella," she called. There was no answer.

She had just inserted the piece of metal into the lock when she saw the door's bronze lever being pushed slowly down again—not rushed or panicked. She froze. A voice in her head screamed, *No!*

Sister Ria stepped back. "Who are you?"

Silence.

The person outside in the garden said, "Open the door." It was a demand now.

Sister Ria did not open the door. She ran from her room, down the hallway, to the back of the hacienda and Aba's quarters. The old woman wasn't there. Sister Ria hurried down the dark passage to her father's room and banged on his door. There was no response there, either. Then she thought she heard something and pressed closer to the door.

"Father?"

From behind her, a voice said, "May I help you?"

She whirled and peered into the darkness of the hallway. Someone was standing near the library door, a dark figure almost lost in the thick shadows. It started walking toward her. Sister Ria backed away, her legs feeling weak.

"I asked you a question, nun," Don Maximiato said.

She did not answer. Instead, she tried to force herself to calm down and studied her father's clothing: a black cape and shirt, black pants and boots, and on his head, a black gaucho hat of the kind that the police had found in Dorothy Regal's room. She was trembling.

"Where have you been?" she asked.

He said nothing.

"Someone is outside in the garden," she said, rushing her words, "they tried to get into my room. I was worried they had broken into your bedroom."

"How touching," he said, stepping closer.

She stepped back. "Was it you?" she asked. Her father took another step toward her, and she matched it with another step backward. She heard footsteps and turned to see the night-duty policeman coming down the hallway. He was carrying a lantern that cast a dull circle of light.

"Is everything all right?" he asked, his voice gruff.

The patrón ignored the man, unlocked the door, and walked into his room, slamming the door behind him and locking it.

Sister Ria banged on it. "Tell me!"

He did not.

She whirled and looked at the policeman. "I need your help," she said. The man followed her down the hall to the rear of the hacienda, where she knocked on Aba's door again.

"What's going on, lady?" the policeman asked.

"Someone tried to get into my room."

He looked a little more alert now.

"They were in the garden."

When there was still no response from Aba's room, she ran to the kitchen, the policeman following. Min and Estrella and the old man who served as the hacienda's night watchman were all asleep. Angel was sitting at the table playing with Fernando.

She shook the others awake and, with lighted lamps and the policeman carrying his pistol, they searched the courtyard and the gardens for the intruder. Fernando joined them, stalking ahead as they moved through the night.

They found no one.

The policeman looked at her. "Nobody out here."

"There was someone. They tried to get into my room."

The man studied her face for a moment, then nodded. "I'm out front if they come again," he said, annoyed at having been awakened, and walked back to the kitchen, headed for his chair in the hacienda's entry hall.

Sister Ria paced anxiously back and forth in the narrow passage in front of Aba's apartment. Min and the others had returned to the kitchen at the far end of the hacienda and would not venture out into the living quarters again that night unless summoned.

Aba, where are you?

Fear building in her chest, she tried the door.

Open.

Fernando shot inside and hopped up onto the small bed and sat. Sister Ria turned in a slow circle and looked at the sparsely furnished compartment, small and filled with nothing but a bed, a chest of drawers, a table and chair. Slowly, she began to struggle with a numbing thought taking shape in the ethers of her mind; she was trying to avoid it.

But she could not. The voices outside her bedroom and in the alley could have been Aba's. "No," she whispered and started to leave. Then she stopped. Her heart was pounding. It was possible. Aba loved her father.

Did she love him so much that she would have killed Dorothy Regal to keep him? Sister Ria closed her eyes and fought the trembling in her body. Had Aba murdered Elsie for the same reason? She had been in the room that night only a short time before the horrible tapping began. She went wherever she wanted inside the hacienda—without anyone questioning.

Sister Ria was having a hard time breathing when she began to search the small room.

Minutes passed slowly until Sister Ria was finally done. She had poked through everything in the compartment, hunting for the book of poems or the brown suit, the black fedora, anything that might implicate the old servant. All the while, she had prayed that she would find nothing. And she had not.

She was on her knees, taking one more look under the mattress and feeling greatly relieved, when Fernando hopped down and walked to the door, his ears forward, staring intently at the crack at the bottom. Sister Ria quickly stood and focused on the doorknob. Her muscles were knotting. Was the intruder still in the house? Was he on the other side of the door? When she could no longer take the waiting, Sister Ria stepped forward and yanked the door open.

Aba stood gazing at her.

Neither of them spoke. Then the old woman looked past her at the things disturbed in her small room.

"I've looked everywhere for you, Aba." Sister Ria paused. "Someone tried to break into my room. I thought perhaps you had been harmed."

"I was out for a walk at the river," Aba said, her eyes moving past Sister Ria to her room again.

"I'm sorry, Aba. I had to know."

"Had to know?"

"Whether or not you had the book."

The old servant looked into her face. "You mean whether I had killed that woman?"

Sister Ria looked down at the floor.

"And did you find it?"

Sister Ria shook her head.

"So then I am not a murderer?"

"Aba—I never really believed—" Sister Ria stopped as if the words had been yanked from her mouth.

Aba was holding the little book out to her. "Is this what you were searching for?"

Sister Ria couldn't find her voice. The book was the companion volume to the one in her pocket.

Aba continued to hold it out to her. "Take it."

Sister Ria did not.

"I assume you are revising your grand murder theories again."

"Where did you find it? I searched his room."

"Are you now back to blaming your father? For the first time in my life, I am ashamed of you, Isadora." Aba tossed the book onto the bed. "It was in plain sight on a table in the sitting room. I picked it up after I found you searching for it in the library and have carried it in my pocket since, knowing if you found it, you would simply blame him again for that woman's murder and stop searching. Which, of course, you are doing right now." She looked into Sister Ria's face. "Unless you have decided I'm a murderer."

"I had hoped it belonged to someone other than my father, Aba."

"That is a lie, Isadora." Aba continued to watch her and then said, "Leave my room, please."

"I'm sorry."

"Leave."

FIVE DAYS

CHAPTER 15

ALL NIGHT LONG Sister Ria sat in a rocking chair on the veranda, thinking about Aba and Dorothy Regal and aching from worry and fatigue. Over and over, she told herself the old servant was not a murderer. How she knew didn't matter. She just knew. But she could not say the same for her father.

As she sat telling herself this, she heard wheels over sand and looked up to see a delivery wagon rolling down the long winding drive. It stopped in front of the house, and she gave up thinking about the two women and sat watching as the driver crawled down and began removing boxes from the bed of the dray.

The man worked without saying anything. Then he brought her a box from the coach and said, "That's all of them."

She pulled on her glasses and read the label.

Mother Superior Isabel at the Benedictine convent in Spain liked to quote the eighteenth-century English poet William Cowper: "Sometimes a light surprises the Christian while he sings; it is the Lord who rises with healing in His wings." As Sister Ria watched the driver walking back to his wagon, she found herself quoting Cowper, too.

She heard a door close behind her and stood and turned around. The patrón was standing on the veranda wearing a U.S. cavalry officer's brown jacket over his nightshirt and an old campaign hat stuffed on his head. He snapped to attention, holding a stiff salute to the brim of his hat like some ancient warrior.

Sister Ria was still looking at her father when the driver asked, "Who's going to give me their signature for these things?"

She just stood staring at her father.

"Hey, lady, I got other stops. You want these or not? Forty boxes of kids' shoes and socks. What are you running, an orphanage?" The man looked at the box in his hand. "Orto-po—"

"Orthopedic," she mumbled.

He had bought shoes for the orphans. He was about to die, and he had ordered the children shoes. One was a corrective shoe for Estrella. Sister Ria could not take her eyes off his face.

✝

That night she stood on the sidewalk in front of the candle shop in town, where she had just purchased thirteen white votives for her father's wake, and looked down at the open telegram in her hand. She felt sick.

She gazed at the words on the page, her head pounding. Clemente Rojo had surprised her by delivering the message that afternoon, saying he happened to be in the telegraph office when it came through. She reread it now for the hundredth time: *Governor will not help. Leave. Danger. Millie.*

Sister Ria shook her head. She would not leave.

Five days.

Sister Ria was starting down the road toward her carriage when she saw it. She stopped and stood gaping up at the large red banner hanging above a clothing store's front door. The store was closed but the front door was open to let the night breeze in. She could see a young woman inside stocking shelves. She read the words on the banner once more, then darted into the store and grabbed the startled girl and dragged her out into the street and pointed up at the sign. "What is that?"

The girl looked frightened. "Sister?"

"Tell me what that means."

The girl studied Sister Ria's face and then the sign, as if she did not understand.

"Tell me!"

The woman tracked Sister Ria's eyes to the banner again: MEN'S CUTAWAYS—ON SALE THIS WEEK.

"A sale—we're having a sale," the girl stammered.

"No, not that. What is a cutaway?"

The girl looked ready to bolt, but Sister Ria held her by the arm. "It's a man's suit, no tails—just a jacket—cut away here," she said, pointing at a spot a few inches below her hip. Sister Ria let go of the girl and stood gazing up at the banner. Without saying anything more, she walked slowly away. The salesgirl was watching her as if she were deranged.

Sister Ria pulled the piece of paper that she had found in Dorothy Regal's room from her pocket and studied it once again: *Brown cutaway.* The curandera's granddaughter had said, "The woman was afraid. Someone had been following her." Sister Ria's throat was tightening. The figure in the brown suit had been following Dorothy Regal.

Now he was following her.

When she started to walk, the idea came full-blown to her, and she returned to her carriage to retrieve the small loaded pistol that Auel always placed beneath the seat whenever she or her father drove at night. The bell in the old town church tolled nine o'clock. She slipped the pistol into her pocket.

The American section of the city was empty, so she headed to the plaza district. Unlike Main Street, La Calle del Negro was packed with people. Mostly men. The night was hot and dry, the street filled with a jarring cacophony of piano and organ music, laughter and shouting. She studied the faces of those who passed her on the sidewalk, hunting with her eyes for the little man in the brown suit, convinced that when she found him, she would find her father. Then—and only then—she would have the proof she needed to rid herself of the doubt in her mind. She had started this search for answers because of her mother and then Aba. But now she was searching for herself.

When she did not find him on La Calle del Negro, she headed for the plaza.

She made a slow circuit around the garden's perimeter, trying to act as if she were simply taking in the night air. Half an hour later, she stopped and picked a handful of white daisies by the path, then waited under one of the gas lamps, knowing that she was clearly visible in the yellow glow and trying to appear unconcerned as her eyes searched for the man in the surrounding darkness. Fifteen minutes later, she began walking again. She saw no one out in the night. Worse, no one followed her. Even so, she felt certain that he was watching her.

She turned into the darkness of the gardens, making herself a more enticing target, moving slowly down a path that cut diagonally through the towering shrubs and trees toward the Pico Hotel. She lingered for a time near the old limestone fountain in the center of the grounds, trying to sort through the night sounds for the tread of footsteps, waiting for him to materialize in the darkness. He did not. Where was he? Surely he knew where she was. She watched a possum scurry across the path in front of her, disappearing in a thick stand of daylilies, as if he had been swallowed by a green sea. An hour passed, and still he had not shown himself. She moved deeper into the heavy foliage.

Sister Ria sat down on a bench under a dark arbor draped with old wisteria that blocked the moonlight and created a small cave in the night. The air was heavy with dew, and she pulled her shawl tighter around her shoulders. She waited.

It did not take long this time.

He came down the path slowly, stopping and turning his head back and forth, searching for her. His careful movements looked sinister in these dark surroundings. She nervously dropped the daisies she was holding and gripped the pistol in her pocket. She was growing frightened. It had been a silly mistake to come here. But she had no choice, she told herself. She had to know. She narrowed her eyes in the dim light as she tried to make out the face of the person approaching in the night. She knew that, dressed in her black habit and sitting in the dense darkness under the arbor, she was almost invisible.

As if he could feel her eyes on him, the man turned slowly on the path until he was staring directly at the arbor. She could tell he had not seen her. He looked confused and turned away again. From the size and shape of the cloaked figure, she guessed it was her father. Suddenly overcome with anger, she stood up from the bench. "I'm here, Father," she snapped, "do you want to kill me?"

The figure whirled. Sister Ria took a step back and sat down hard on the bench. It was not her father.

Clemente Rojo was holding his little silver revolver in one hand. "Good Sister," he said, tipping his head, "praise God you're okay."

"You were following me," she said.

"Yes."

"Why?"

"I saw you walking alone around the plaza. It's not safe."

"I grew up in this pueblo," she said stiffly.

"Yes. But Los Angeles is now a very dangerous place." He stepped into the darkness of the arbor, blocking her exit to the path, the revolver at his side. "People are murdered in these gardens. I would not want that to happen to you."

Sister Ria's heart was thumping against the wall of her chest. She remembered that he had followed her into the alley the night she had heard the child's voice calling out to her; he had also brought her Milagros's telegram. And now he was here. "You carry a pistol—"

"Yes, Los Angeles is a dangerous place," he repeated softly, and stepped closer to her.

Sister Ria cocked the pistol in her pocket but didn't take it out. "I must go," she said. "Don Vargas is waiting for me at the hotel. I'm sure he is looking for me now."

"You must be mistaken. Don Vargas is at his home, resting—he is an old man."

"No, he is waiting for me," she lied.

"You sound frightened."

"You startled me, that's all." She took a step forward.

Clemente did not move to let her pass.

She was about to step around him when she heard the sound of voices. The editor turned and watched as a young couple strolled down the path. Sister Ria didn't hesitate. She walked out of the arbor and trailed closely behind the man and woman until she reached Olive Street. Clemente followed along behind them.

"Good night, Sister," he called, "stay safe."

Sister Ria hurried to La Calle del Negro, shaken by her encounter with Clemente Rojo. Had he truly stumbled upon her by accident as she walked around the plaza, or had he been following her? There seemed to be too many coincidences connected to him. Was he somehow involved? Millie had told her to trust no one. Still, he could simply be a newspaperman out at night, walking around looking for news, carrying a pistol because the town was indeed dangerous.

She walked on, returning to her hunt for the man in the brown suit.

After looking up and down both sides of the street, she turned to the windows, peering into each establishment as she passed, searching the people's faces inside. Nothing.

Strand's Road was a few yards in front of her. A man was urinating against a brick wall. She turned away and waited for him to finish, then moved into the lighted passageway. While it was not as crowded as La Calle del Negro, a number of men and women were moving in both directions over its bricked surface. She started up the narrow road.

At the top, she stopped and took a long, close look at the building. The structure appeared to have been a handsome home once. There was nothing that designated it as a house of prostitution—just a small black hand-lettered sign over the front door: LA FIESTA. The glass in the windows had been painted black. There were three carriages tied up outside. She forced her thoughts back to the reason she had come: to find her father dressed in the brown suit. She had hoped to find him walking up Strand's Road or standing outside the building. She wasn't about to go looking for him inside. Perhaps if she waited, he would come out the door or up the street. It was as good as any of her other ideas.

She leaned back against a brick fence on the opposite side of the road and stood worrying over her fears about him. Gazing at the side staircase that led to Dorothy Regal's small apartment, Sister Ria wondered if she had missed something in that room. She fought the urge to go back. Then a heavy blanket of fatigue draped over her, and she closed her eyes.

The figure in the brown suit was on her fast.

He had come out of the shadows and knocked her to the ground with a blow from a blackjack that momentarily dazed her. Then he dragged her through an open gate into a small fenced enclosure filled with stacks of lumber. She pulled the pistol from her pocket and rolled to face her attacker, but something collided with her skull, and the world spun dangerously out of control. It was over. Her thoughts blotted out into darkness.

Through the fog drifting behind her eyes, she heard Milagros telling her to move, to get away, and she rolled through a puddle of muddy water, clawing desperately at the dirt, trying to escape. But her efforts were weak, her body out of control. Then someone was ordering her to keep quiet or she'd be killed. She was no longer holding the little pistol.

The whine started deep in the pit of her.

"Shut up," the voice snapped, and a fist slammed into her head, the blow driving the side of her face into the dirt. Blood spurted from her nose, and the world went silent. The only thing she heard was a small clear voice somewhere deep in her brain: Milagros calling to her to play in the surf. It was warm and sunny . . . and safe.

She was on her back, sliding into dark nothingness.

When she came to moments later, she thought she had been buried alive before she realized her habit had been pulled over her head.

"You will not!" she shrieked.

The figure hit her again, the blow driving her deeper into unconsciousness. Instinctively, after years of brawling with street children, she fought back, clawing and trying to bite through the thick material of her habit.

"You will not touch me!" she screamed. She began to drift into a senseless haze. The sound came to her from somewhere in the dark emptiness of her mind: the same hard, cold snap of metal that she had heard that night in her bedroom. She screamed louder.

Then there was the sound of people running up the alley, and lantern light was bouncing in the night, and her attacker leaped away into the darkness.

When she had gotten control over the spasms in her body, Sister Ria crawled to her feet and looked down at the mud covering her habit and made a weak attempt to get it off. She sat down hard on the ground. The small crowd of men who had rescued her simply stood and watched her sitting, her arms and legs akimbo, looking badly out of sorts. They were decent enough men, they just didn't know what was the right thing to do with a nun who they believed had almost been raped, and so they just stood and watched her.

"You okay, ma'am?" one of them asked.

She nodded but didn't move. At last, two of them helped her to her feet and walked her slowly out of the fenced enclosure to the alley in front of the brothel. The small crowd was respectfully quiet. After a while someone asked, "You got a carriage somewhere, ma'am?" She merely gazed into the man's face.

Then a canvas-topped surrey pulled up, and the driver said, "I'll take her home."

She was wobbling on her feet, and the men struggled to politely push her up into the backseat before pulling the curtains closed around her. "You sure you're okay?" one of the men asked, sticking his head in through the split in the side curtain. "We can get a doctor if you want."

She shook her head and wiped blood from her nose onto her sleeve, then leaned back into the seat and closed her eyes. Her head was pounding, and she still felt dazed. A curtain separated her from the front seat, and she listened as the driver clucked the carriage horse up Strand's Road, away from the brothel and La Calle del Negro.

The night had been hot and dry until a rain squall blew in from the Pacific. The water pounded hard on the canvas roof. Sister Ria's head was clearing, and she focused on the sound of the pelting rain. The overhang of the surrey roof would offer some cover to the driver, but she knew the downpour, driven by the wind, would still be getting into where the man sat. "I'm sorry about the rain," she called through the curtain. The pain in her head soared, and she stopped talking. The driver said something, but she couldn't make it out in the storm.

She leaned back and ran a finger gingerly over her teeth and jaw to confirm that nothing was broken. Finished, she checked her arms and fingers, then her ribs. Again, nothing felt worse than sore. She looked around in the darkness of the cabin, her eyes focusing on a small brass plaque on one of the doors that read BRADFORD'S LIVERY. The surrey was rented.

Sister Ria was about to offer money to cover the rental when her nose began to bleed again. She tipped her head back and called out to the driver, "Pardon me. Do you have a rag I can use to stop a nosebleed?" The rain had momentarily stopped, and she listened as the driver pulled a canvas tool bag from under the seat. Then the road suddenly became rougher, the surrey hitting ruts and rocks, and she glanced out the side curtain. They were headed for the dark foothills of the Santa Monica Mountains.

"We've made a wrong turn," Sister Ria called.

There was no answer.

"Sir?"

An arm in the sleeve of a brown suit came slashing back through the curtain, the blade of the knife slicing the air, catching material, cutting deeply into the darkness of the cabin. Then the driver whirled around and yanked aside the curtains and stared at the empty seat.

The side door was open.

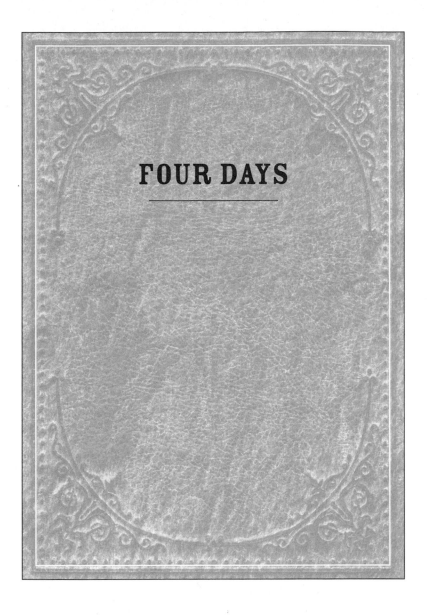

FOUR DAYS

CHAPTER 16

HAVING ESCAPED THE CARRIAGE moments before the attack, Sister Ria had hidden in the thick chaparral at the side of the road and watched through a screen of manzanita leaves, rain, and darkness as the man in the brown suit stood up on the surrey's seat in the drenching rain, searching the surrounding darkness for her. She couldn't see much of anything from her hiding place. But whoever it was, he was frighteningly determined. He had waited for almost two hours for her to move before he finally gave up and drove back toward town.

When she was certain he was gone, Sister Ria had run through the rainy night for home, following the old sheep trail that ran some twenty-five yards south of the main road.

She had been too afraid to go into the hacienda and instead waited out the night in the garden, watching the house. She saw no one. But she knew now that the figure in the brown suit was not just following her. He wanted her dead like Dorothy Regal.

At first light, she slipped into the house and changed into the habit that Aba had had made for her. Still frightened but feeling better physically, she hurried down the loggia toward his room, listening to the sounds of things being moved, of clanging and banging.

Rounding the corner, she jerked to a halt. The wide hallway outside her father's room was a jumbled mess of furniture, personal belongings, pails, brooms, and mops. Servants were hurrying in and out, once again removing the animals' pens from the patrón's bedroom. The same pens they had removed two days before. She shook her head. He never gave in.

She studied him from a distance. Had he tried to kill her the night before? She found it hard to believe. He looked like a shriveled Egyptian merchant in the middle of a flea market.

Don Maximiato was sitting in a large leather chair in the center of the hallway, dressed in a Turkish bathrobe, a fez with a long black tassel stuck on top of his head, the tassel falling in front of his face. He slapped at it as if it were an annoying fly. There were a number of street children sitting at his feet. Angel María was holding Fernando in her lap.

"You treat me as if I am a child," he yelled at Aba. The children giggled.

Aba appeared in the doorway, looking down sternly at the old man. "*Silencio,*" she said to the children, and then to the patrón, "You have made the room filthy again."

Min appeared, wearing a beautiful red silk Chinese robe, the long wide sleeves rolled up, a green ribbon tied in his pigtail. He was carrying a stack of papers that he set down, at Aba's direction, on the hallway floor. Then he quickly returned to the room. He looked sad, as if he were the only one who realized what was about to happen.

Don Maximiato began chuckling. Aba watched him for a moment, then shook her head and disappeared into the room. The patrón leaned back and shut his eyes, something reptilian in his look. The children sat watching him, waiting for him to say something funny or to start a new game.

Sister Ria knelt beside him. "Father."

He opened one eye.

"The time is near."

He tipped his head and looked at her clothing. "Why do you dress like that?"

"Because I am a nun."

"No—to annoy me." He licked his lips and said, "Your face is bruised."

"Yes."

He smiled an odd twisted smile and leaned over and touched the top of her veil. Then he pressed his thumb into her forehead and made the sign of the cross on her skin. "Do you wish me to pray for you?"

"No, Father, pray for yourself."

He said nothing, just picked up a cigarette from a small table and lit it on a burning candle, continuing to stare at her face.

She stood shaking her head in sadness. To her surprise, she was overcome with grief for the fate of this man. Sister Ria cleared her throat. "Is there anything I can do for you?"

He picked a piece of ash from the tip of his tongue and took another draw on the cigarette and blew a cloud of smoke into her face. "Yes," he said.

She leaned closer to him. "What, Father?"

"Trade me your outfit. I have made you a perfectly good offer."

Tears welled in her eyes. Not even the closeness of his own death could frighten him into reality.

Sister Ria was walking down the hallway toward her bedroom, when Angel María ran up alongside and grasped her hand. Fernando trailed along behind the girl.

"Good morning, María," Sister Ria said. María looked worried. "Is everything okay?"

The girl just stared up at her.

"María?"

"Are you going away?"

Sister Ria stopped and squatted and took hold of both of María's hands. "Why do you ask?"

María sniffed. "You told the patrón the time is near. You're going to leave. Aren't you?" Tears were running down the girl's cheeks. "You shouldn't go."

Sister Ria pulled María in tight to her. "I'll have to leave at some time, María. I work for God and he will want me to come home."

María shook her head hard. "This is your home and God shouldn't take you from it. You need to be my mother."

Sister Ria slid to her knees and pulled María onto her lap and rocked back and forth with the girl held tightly in her arms. "María, María, María. I'm a nun. As much as I would truly love to, I can't be your mother." Sister Ria waited a moment and then said, "Did you know her?"

María shook her head again. "No. I didn't ever see her. And I don't care what you are. If you leave, you must take me with you. Promise." María was sobbing without sound.

"Ohhh, María. How can I promise you that?"

"You must."

"But how can I?"

"I don't know how," María cried, "I just know you have to."

Fernando stared at Sister Ria with his one good eye. He looked thoroughly ashamed of her.

✝

The old plaza church looked different. Sister Ria gazed up at a European-style belfry that had been added onto one side of the edifice; steep marble steps rose in front of her, leading to heavy carved double doors. There was something off-putting about these changes.

To her left stood a tall adobe wall, some thirteen feet high, covered with a veneer of fresh white plaster: the garden wall of saints. She went through its open doorway into an enclosed courtyard with formal pathways, fountains, and dark hidden pockets amid lush greenery.

She moved slowly through the garden, listening to the splashing of water, smelling the rich tang of orange blossoms, and feeling that the humble old church and this exquisite garden did not belong together. She pulled on the heavy sanctuary door and slipped inside, reluctant in a way she understood but didn't want to face. The church reminded her of the small medieval cathedrals in the southern regions of Spain, beautiful in its stark simplicity. It had been built in 1822, with crude tools and simple materials, by the tireless labor of Franciscan Indian neophytes. The church of her childhood—but, like everything else in her life, forever changed.

The high ceiling was still supported by the same dark rough-hewn beams, but now there were lovely brass chandeliers hanging from the central beam, and the thick walls gleamed the stark bone white of fresh plaster. The altar was new, built of gleaming woods, replacing the rough adobe platform of her youth. The rows of benches were also gone; instead, there were oak pews padded with red velvet cushions. Even the old uneven floor had been replaced by heavy red tile polished to a brilliant sheen.

The rough wooden plaques in Spanish commemorating the stations of the cross that, as a child, Sister Ria had lovingly run her hands over a thousand times were now white marble slabs, the sacred words chiseled into the cold hard stone in English.

She was praying when a door opened at the rear of the sanctuary and a tall, thin priest in a white cassock, a silver crucifix dangling from his corded waist, appeared with a well-dressed American woman at his side. They were deep in conversation about a wedding, the priest laughing at something the woman had said, and he did not notice Sister Ria at first as they approached down the aisle. The priest was smoking a cigarette, his accent French, his English excellent.

Then he saw her and stopped and looked at her as if surprised that anyone would stand in this church without his permission. The American woman continued past.

"May I help you?" the priest asked in Spanish. His tone was quietly arrogant.

It seemed an odd question from a priest to a nun of his faith. The man's pale face was screened in a thin veil of smoke.

"Is Father Guevera here?" she asked.

He raised the cigarette to his lips and took a draw and held it, studying her. He did not look pleased to see her here. The American woman had walked on toward the front doors.

"I will be back," the priest said to Sister Ria, hurrying after the woman.

Nervous, Sister Ria watched him. He was perhaps forty, but something about him seemed much older, and he did not look healthy. He talked for a moment to the woman, laughing and gesturing, then they both looked at her, the woman nodding at something the priest had said. After a few more minutes of conversation, the priest kissed the woman's hand, and she left.

He returned down the aisle. "Madrid," he said to her. "Father Guevera has been in Madrid for some seven years. He is sick, perhaps dead." There was no feeling to the words.

"Monsignor Abel?"

"He left this morning for Santa Barbara." The man waited for her to say something. When she didn't, he took another pull on what was left of his cigarette and then let it drop to the floor, where he put it out with his sandal. "You are the Mexican nun. Your father is Maximiato Lugo."

"Spanish nun, but yes. I have come to ask you to hear his confession and to prepare him for death."

The man waited.

"I lived here in the pueblo once," she said, feeling awkward. "This was our church. My grandfather helped construct it, my parents married in it, and I—"

He held up his hand, the gesture indicating that he did not want to have this conversation with her. "I have heard of you—of your father." He paused. "He has created his own church, and he has been convicted of murder. I cannot bless such a man or administer the last rites."

She glanced around her. "The sanctuary is very beautiful," she said, "different from when I worshipped here."

"Yes. Now how else may I be of service to you?"

"The Mexican people believe this is no longer their church—that is the reason my father expanded our family chapel. That is not a sin. You must bless him."

The priest shook his head. "Is there anything else?"

"You must," she repeated, more desperately this time. A moment later, she added, "An unborn fetus—"

"I have heard that also," he said, interrupting her again. "An unborn stained by sin—never baptized." He was shaking his head.

"The child needs to be given the last rites of burial as well."

"Impossible."

"It is just a child," she said emphatically.

"Satan's child."

"No, just a little unborn child." Her voice was rising. "Who never had a chance at the life God had given it. And my father needs to be brought to God at his final hour."

The priest gazed off at the altar as if lost in his own thoughts, then caught himself and looked back at her. "You, a nun of all people, should know that I cannot sanctify this child's or your father's soul."

She stared at the heavy golden cross that stood on the altar. "There are orphaned children at the Lugo hacienda. My father has been caring for them. The church will need to take over their care."

The priest just continued to look at her.

"Did you hear me, Father?"

"We are not a wealthy church." He waved his hand over the sanctuary. "We have just remodeled the entire structure, making God's church beautiful. It was very costly. And we have added the lovely prayer garden."

Sister Ria's anger was rising in her throat. "I don't care how beautiful you have made your church. There are children who need care. And I believe that is the responsibility of the church."

"I suggest you worry about what you believe, nun."

Sister Ria turned on her heel and walked toward the rear of the church. She turned back and asked, "Do you know where the child's mother is buried?"

The priest looked surprised. "You don't know?" He lit another cigarette.

"No."

He took a long draw on the cigarette, blowing the smoke out through his nostrils and looking pleased with himself. "Your family cemetery. Making it unholy ground."

Sister Ria smothered her surprise. "Thank you." She started again for the rear of the church.

"Nun," the man said sharply.

Sister Ria stopped but did not turn around. "Yes?"

"Stay away from that woman and this unborn creature as well— unless you wish to join your father in damnation," he said.

"And you may go to hell as well, priest."

The candelabra was burning in her father's bedroom when she knocked and pushed the door open and walked inside. He was dressed in a woman's silk kimono with a bright red obi around his waist, sitting cross-legged on the bed, his eyes closed, his palms turned upward, his lips moving silently. She waited. The sharp smell of carbolic acid mixing with burning incense filled her nostrils and made her sneeze. If he heard, he did not move.

When he seemed to have stopped praying, she said, "Father, we must bury the child."

✝

The deep hole had been dug next to her mother's grave. His grave. She stood in the fading cadmium light of the California dusk, looking down at the dark cavity in the earth, her body trembling, her breath jerking in her throat. She could hear the familiar sound of a covey of Gambel's quail calling to one another in the chaparral higher up the hillside, and thought of the hundreds of times she had walked these same hills with him, discussing crops and livestock. Why had they not loved each other? She had no answer.

Slowly, she gained control over herself and placed a hand on her mother's gravestone and watched the old women who worked in the kitchen struggling up the mountain, their heads draped in black shawls, bearing baskets of roses that they began to place around a smaller hole a few yards down the hill. The women were moaning and crying, and she was swept up in their grief.

Her eyes moved to a fresh mound of earth beside the tiny grave. The French priest had been right: Dorothy Regal was buried on the gentle south-facing slope of the hill behind the hacienda. Sister Ria bent and kissed her mother's gravestone and then walked over and put a hand on Dorothy Regal's wooden cross. Remembering the priest's warning that the woman was unclean, Sister Ria was struck by the kindness behind the act of bringing this woman—whom the Church had condemned to hell, whom the Church would not bury—to this place. She would never understand him fully, would never quite grasp the great swings of his emotions, the confusing dichotomy of his enormous sensitivity interrupted by irrational bursts of anger and cruelty. She had no idea whether he was a murderer.

It no longer seemed to matter.

The women had finished placing the roses around the edges of the tiny grave when the others arrived. It was a solemn procession. Don Maximiato came first, wearing a spotless white satin alb fringed in purple and gathered at the waist, the miter of a Catholic bishop on his head. He walked slowly, carrying a long wooden staff tipped with a golden cross; three young Indian boys followed him in the brown robes and straw sandals of acolytes. The small group was trailed by the familiar gathering of street urchins. Little Angel María followed a few yards behind, Fernando at her side. Sister Ria smiled. There was something very right about the procession, sanctified or not. Then she saw Auel carrying a beautiful miniature rosewood coffin, the size of a shoe box, and she clasped her hands in front of her. Min, Estrella, Cristina, and the other mourners followed. Aba was not among them.

The service was not long. Her father conducted it in the ancient Latin text of the Church. She knew the sacred words of the commitment of the dead to the earth by heart and wondered where he had learned them in such wonderfully precise form. He stood before the grave, the little coffin resting on a bed of white roses, and spoke the hallowed words crisply and with a depth of feeling that reached deep into her heart, surprising her greatly.

The man possessed a grand theatrical side, she told herself, then shook her head. Whatever he did, be it addle-headed or cruel, he passionately believed. She listened to the old Roman words spilling out into the dry air, drifting through the evening light as if they might drift on forever. Even to God.

It was almost dark, the ceremony at a close. She watched as he bent and placed his hands on the coffin, sweat running down his face. Gently, he patted the wood as if touching the head of a living child. "Lord, we commend this sinless soul to your forgiving grace. Joyous that she will grow up in your heaven." Sister Ria smiled through her tears and nodded. Then Auel and Min began to lower the coffin into the earth.

She continued to watch him. The final words had been his, not those of the Church. And they had been exactly right—words the priest at the plaza church should have spoken here. Sister Ria walked to her father's side. He was gazing into the grave, and she wondered what he saw, whether he was seeing his own life spilling down into the dark hole, at last coming to grips with his approaching end.

"Father?"

He continued looking down.

"Thank you," she said.

He did not respond.

Auel removed the purple cloth from the child's headstone, folded it carefully, and handed it to one of the women, then placed the bottom edge of the small marble tablet into a slit in the earth at the head of the grave. Sister Ria took a deep breath and exhaled slowly. Her father had thought of everything right and good. Sister Ria crossed herself and knelt before the stone and looked at its smooth surface.

Her eyes moved quickly over the chiseled letters, then back again. She gasped for air. The inscription read:

Isadora Victorine Lugo
1854–1871

She whirled to face him, but he was walking away. The boy, Min, was at his side, carrying a large black bag. She turned back to the grave. His insane cruelty would damn him, she told herself, her eyes locked on the second date chiseled into the smooth surface of the stone: the year she had fled. She ran after him. "How dare you!"

Min jumped away from her father when she shouted, and he held the black bag nervously in both hands, staring at her as though she were mad.

"Your insane games mean nothing to me. But to demean the child? Have you no decency?"

Don Maximiato stopped walking and looked at her.

"You put my name on the child's gravestone!"

He raised his eyebrows. "Your name? Isadora Victorine Lugo?"

She cleared her throat. "You know what I mean."

"Your name is something silly, like Hister Lea. Is it not?"

"Do not bait me, please!"

"The Isadora Victorine Lugo I knew died in 1871, just as the stone reads."

"I did not die."

"And you are not Isadora Victorine Lugo." He crossed himself mockingly, then continued to walk slowly down the service road.

She started to go after him but Angel María grabbed her hand and pulled her back.

Don Maximiato spent the next two hours doctoring the poor Mexicans and Indians who stood lined up in front of the empty work sheds serving as temporary examining rooms and, for the sickest patients, as wards with small cots. Sister Ria watched him work, silently fuming. Min had helped him into a clean white doctor's smock, tying his priestly cincture and crucifix around his waist, and he was moving quickly and efficiently through the line of waiting patients, listening with a stethoscope to one man's chest, peering into mouths, eyes, and ears, probing with his fingers. Grudgingly, she began to sense that his medical technique and decisions were as good as those of the doctors she had worked with over the years in India.

Wounds were properly cleaned and sutured using the latest accepted procedures, teeth pulled, bones set, drugs administered. How he had learned to do all of this, she didn't know. But he had obviously trained himself to understand the body and medicine, the available pharmacology. She thought of the small book on dissection. It made sense now. And she could see that he offered much more than medicine to these people, administering blessings, brief prayers, advice, and coins that Min handed to him from the black bag.

The people gazed upon him as though he were truly sainted, and for a moment she understood what Auel had said about him. Then the hurt and anger returned, and all thoughts of sainthood disappeared.

She followed along behind him, angrily looking for a chance to reengage him in verbal battle. But as the line of waiting sick and injured grew, something tugged at her heart, and she gave up wanting to fight with him and joined in the work. Quickly, she separated those most seriously ill from the others, leaving the first for him and moving by herself through the rest. He did not object, except to have Min give her a smock to wear. When she had finished with her group of patients, she joined him, preparing medicines as he directed, bandaging and cleaning wounds. They worked silently side by side for three more hours. They hadn't worked this way in eleven years. Oddly, she thought, it felt right somehow. Slowly, the sadness she had felt earlier replaced her anger.

It was dark and growing late, the rooms lit by lanterns and candles. They had seen the last patient, and the kitchen maids were bringing trays of food and drink and setting them on tables in front of the workrooms. Swarms of children gathered around the food. Two young Mexican women dressed as nurses in clean uniforms were assisting those who needed help to eat and drink. Min was asleep on one of the cots.

Her father rested on a bench, holding a cigarette in his thin hand, squinting against the drifting smoke. She was sitting on the ground holding María on her lap. María was asleep and Sister Ria was sipping chilled orange juice from a glass and watching him. She had no idea what to think about this man. Perhaps what she had once believed was madness was simply delusion. Whatever his illness, he vacillated between warped illusions of reality and crystal-clear lucidity. She no longer hated him. She wasn't certain what she felt. Pity, perhaps.

Don Maximiato looked up when Sister Ria's shadow fell across him. "Are there more?"

"No, Father. We are done," she said, holding the still sleeping María on her hip.

He nodded and took a pull on his cigarette, then broke into a hacking cough.

When he finally stopped, she said, "Please—"

"No."

Sister Ria nodded and sat down on the bench with María in her arms and leaned in to the wall and closed her eyes, exhausted.

THREE DAYS

CHAPTER 17

WORN DOWN by her constant worrying, Sister Ria had fallen into a deep sleep that had carried her, tossing and turning, through the morning and into the afternoon of the following day. When she awoke, Aba was sitting next to the bed in her room. The old servant nodded at her and then helped her dress. Neither of them said anything until Sister Ria started for the door of her bedroom.

"There's—"

Sister Ria turned back and studied the old servant's face. Aba, too, looked exhausted. "Aba?"

"There's nothing more you can do for him. I'm sorry I asked you to try."

Sister Ria just looked at her.

Aba shook her head. "It's time to let him go." The old servant stared at the material of Sister Ria's habit as if looking through it at something else. Then she refocused her eyes on Sister Ria's face. "Your dream. The patrón did not live his. Live yours. Walk from this."

Sister Ria shook her head. "My dream no longer matters."

Aba stepped forward and straightened the material of Sister Ria's habit. Then she put a hand under Sister Ria's chin, raising it slightly. "Stand up straight, child," she said stiffly. "You are the daughter of the patrón. Have you forgotten all that I taught you?"

Sister Ria smiled at the old familiar line. "No," she said. "I have not forgotten."

Aba nodded. "Good. Then do as I have told you."

✝

José Vargas was sitting in a large leather chair writing a letter when a servant brought Sister Ria into the room. Vargas did not appear surprised to see her. He smiled warmly and motioned her to a nearby chair.

"I didn't know where else to go," she said.

"You are always welcome in my home, child."

"Tell me what I should do."

"Child?"

She took a breath. "I don't know what to do."

José Vargas studied her face for a moment longer. He set the letter he was writing down on a side table and called, "Antonio."

The servant reappeared in the doorway. "Señor Vargas?"

"Café for the good sister."

Vargas waited and then said, "You and your sister have tried very hard."

Antonio returned, carrying a tray with coffee and sweet cakes that he set on a nearby table. He poured a cup for her. She waited for him to leave the room, gazing at the floor. Vargas just watched her.

She looked up at the man as if she had just realized he was in the room and said, "Don José, you must help me. Please."

The old man shook his head. "I am truly sorry." He seemed to nod off in his chair.

"Don José, please."

The old man stirred and sat up straighter and picked up the guitar leaning against his chair. He strummed it softly, changing chords with his thick fingers, gazing off into the shadows as if remembering other times. "After you and Milagros had left, I told Don Maximiato to leave this place, to paint his sunsets. He still owns the Lugo ancestral home in Sevilla." He stopped playing the instrument. "But always he would ask me: 'Who shall care for La Cienega and the children?' And I never had an answer—not after you were gone."

She gazed down at her hands and then, as if talking to herself, she said, "He loves the children very much."

"The street children?"

"Yes."

The old man smiled. "After the death of your mother, he turned to prostitutes for solace." Vargas slowly shook his head. "And now he believes that all the wandering children of Los Angeles are his own." He chuckled and began to softly strum the strings of the guitar again.

Sister Ria thought of Dorothy Regal and her dead child and

shivered in the heat of the room. She looked at the old man and said again, "Don José, tell me what I should do."

He put his hand over the guitar strings, and the sound stopped. "Isadora, you must consider things as they are."

She waited.

"Your father will die—there is nothing you or I can do for him. You must face that reality."

She fought to catch her breath.

Don Vargas watched her in the weak light for a time before he said, "The offer from the gas company was generous. The Americans control everything. They own almost everything."

"I don't care," she said. "Tell me you will try to help."

"You are a young woman. Take their offer—the money from the sale, along with profits from—"

"Tell me," she repeated.

"If there are things you do not like in the agreement, I will negotiate changes. Do it, Isadora."

"Tell me!"

Don José shook his head slowly and said, "I cannot."

Sister Ria was standing next to the table where Don Vargas had laid the letter he was writing. Tears welled in her eyes. She wiped them on the heels of her hands and looked down at the paper and jumped. She read the words again slowly: *May you pardon my intrusion.* Her hands were trembling. It was the phrase on the cable sent to her in India. Don José was strumming the guitar again.

"You sent it?" she said.

Don Vargas looked up from the instrument. "Sent what, child?"

"The cable telling me of the murder."

The old man studied her face and then nodded. "Yes. I did. You are my godchild—would you expect me to do less?"

Sister Ria was watching his face closely. "How did you know where I was?"

The old man smiled at her as if she had told him a joke. "It's a small world."

"No, tell me. How did you find me?"

Don Vargas took a drink from his coffee. "You had run away twice, child, to become a nun. When you disappeared the third time, I sent a letter to a friend who is a cardinal and asked for his assistance in finding you." He put the cup down. "It took about a year until I was told you were in Spain. When your father was arrested, I contacted a Mother Superior Isabel—that is the correct name, isn't it?"

She nodded.

"She informed me that you were working in a convent hospital in India."

Sister Ria straightened the material of her habit over her knees and then looked up at Don Vargas and said, "You didn't sign it."

He shrugged.

It was late evening, and the traffic on the streets of town was beginning to lighten. Sister Ria was moving in a daze, her conversation with Don Vargas running itself over and over in her mind. She was wondering how he fit in all of this. Could he—her godfather and Don Maximiato's closest friend—have helped condemn the patrón to death? She gazed blindly down the empty street.

His insistence that she sell La Brea to the gas company troubled her deeply. Slowly, the disturbing thought took full shape in her mind: Don Vargas had sold himself. She was convinced that he had sent her the cable so that she would return from India and sign over the land to the gas company. She fought off the thought. He could have been simply trying to do what was best for her. He was not only her godfather but also her family's attorney. And he was her father's friend. She closed her eyes.

He could not be her father's Judas.

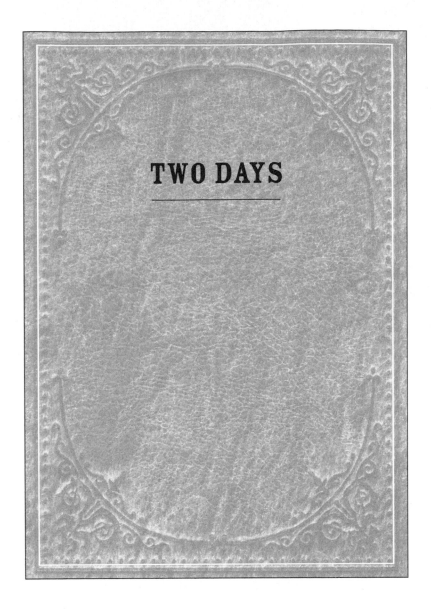

TWO DAYS

CHAPTER 18

THE DAWN HAD materialized without her noticing, stealing silently over the beach like a ghost. Sister Ria was sitting in the sand with her knees tucked up under her chin, watching the light break over the ocean, waves exploding in a roaring roll toward the empty shore as if the water would never stop rushing forward. Plovers scurried across the wet sand, fleeing from the onrushing surge of water, and when it receded, they chased after it as if they had lost something valuable in the waves. She could see the dark smooth heads of sea otters out beyond the breakers—hunting abalone in the rocks below—and a line of brown pelicans slowly flapping their way north over the surf. Every so often one of the big birds would plunge from the line, diving into the sea as if it had been shot, only to rise flapping out of the foaming waters moments later with a fish in its beak. "Bless Thy creation, Lord," she whispered.

The shore was empty, stretching miles in both directions. A small driftwood fire warmed her back. She had not spent the night in this place by accident. When she was seventeen, her father had brought her here so he could paint. It was the only time they had gone anywhere together other than town. And she did not know why they had done so.

He had just asked her to accompany him, as if he had something important to say to her. But he had said nothing. He had simply set up his easel and painted all day and into the evening. When he was done, he had handed her the painting. It was a lovely seascape, with her sitting on the sand and looking out at the far horizon, the sunlight on her. It was the only time he had ever painted her. She had said nothing, had just stood and looked at the wet oils until the scene blurred before her eyes. She had then tried to hand him the painting back, but he would not take it.

Aba had the Chinese carpenters who worked in the thatched shed behind the stables build a gilded frame for the painting and then had it hung in the long hallway of the hacienda, where the light from a south-facing window would illuminate it, as if it were precious.

On the night Isadora ran away, she removed the small painting from its place on the wall and took it with her, carried it wrapped in brown paper for three months, over five thousand miles, and did not know why. All she knew was that she wanted it. No—needed it. She had hung it in her cell at the monastery. It didn't matter why.

✝

Sundown at the hacienda had always been Sister Ria's favorite time: the cool dry breezes, the sweet smell of night jasmine, smears of lamplight on dead-white plaster, the river whispering as if it wanted to tell her something. But there was nothing to love about this evening.

She was sitting in a rocker on the veranda next to her father, a thin film of sweat covering her skin, her thoughts focused on the pocket in the sand dunes where they had sat together. Don Maximiato coughed. She looked at him. He was sitting in a chair, sketching the chickens scratching for the corn he had tossed into the dirt at the porch edge. He was making sketch after sketch, his hand moving so fast over the paper that it looked as if he were trying to pack a lifetime of drawing into one evening.

She fought back the tears and shook her head. He wore a Mexican general's dress uniform with a purple sash and a fine silver sword. She smiled at the outlandish outfit. It was the first time in her life she had ever done that: smile fondly at his craziness.

They had been sitting in silence for the past hour. For all she knew, he was not even aware that she was next to him. There was a growing pile of crumpled papers beside his chair. Then Min came out of the house, approaching slowly in his mincing shuffle, bowing up and down as he came, smiling his forever smile. As before, she could see the sadness in the boy's features. He stopped a few feet from the patrón, bowed deeply, and held the position.

The old man did not respond. He just continued drawing.

Min waited, bent over. Finally, he moved forward a few inches and cleared his throat.

Sister Ria was stunned by her father's quickness as he exploded like a coiled snake, knocking his chair backward and tossing his sketchbook out into the yard, scattering frightened chickens. Slowly, he turned toward the young servant, his hand moving toward the hilt of his sword.

Min was backing and bowing his way toward the house.

"I have told you before, do not disturb me when I am working."

"Father—" Sister Ria started.

"You be quiet!" he yelled, whirling and glaring at her. He turned back to the frightened boy. "Do you not know who I am?" he shouted.

Sister Ria was moving to stop him when Aba appeared in the doorway. "Don Maximiato," she said firmly, her voice snapping like a flag in wind.

The old man looked at her, hesitated, and stood glaring at the bent-over back of Min. Aba watched him for a moment longer, to be sure the tirade was over, and then nodded deferentially and picked up the chair and sketchbook.

The patrón turned toward her. "Have the children been fed?"

"Of course, Don Maximiato," she said, her voice carefully modulated, once again the respectful head servant.

Aba took him by the arm and guided him back to his chair and handed him his sketchbook, dusting it carefully with her apron before she let it go. The patrón pulled a new charcoal pencil from his fine military coat and resumed his frantic sketching, this time of Min's frightened face.

It was fully dark when the horse and surrey came down the long drive and stopped in front of the veranda, where Sister Ria and her father were still sitting. Don Maximiato continued to sketch. He did not look up. The servants had lit the lantern sconces on the hacienda walls an hour earlier, and these were casting a weak light on the faces of Dr. Reed Johnson and José Vargas in the surrey. The men nodded at Sister Ria.

"Gentlemen," she said. The patrón did not acknowledge them.

"We have come to speak with Don Maximiato," Vargas said, struggling down from the buggy.

Sister Ria stood. "I'll leave you." Her voice was cold. She was still not certain what to think of Don Vargas.

Aba had stepped out onto the veranda and stood a few feet away, tall and straight, a black shawl over her shoulders, her thin hands clasped in front of her.

"No," Vargas said to Sister Ria, "you should hear this." The old lawyer was using a cane, and he hobbled up onto the veranda in front of Don Maximiato. He stood looking down at his old friend. Don Maximiato continued to ignore him, staring out now into the darkness of the yard as if he were the only person alive in the world. Vargas stepped closer and touched the patrón's shoulder, then brought the hand tenderly to his face. "Maxie. It's José Vargas. I've come to tell you that everything legal has been completed and signed by the officials of the city and the state to allow the execution to proceed. I have been asked by the district court of Los Angeles to read you the following order of your execution."

Sister Ria thought that Aba had taken a step backward at the words, but she was not certain. The old woman was standing with her chin elevated slightly, her eyes locked on the patrón. Vargas began to read, but Sister Ria was no longer hearing him. Her mind was being swept along by a brutal flood of memories: hacienda mornings, Milagros, coffee and chocolates, foreign newspapers, arguments, grape harvests. Her breath was jerking in her throat. She stepped up behind her father's chair and put her hands on his shoulders and squeezed slightly. He did not move. Vargas finished.

"Don Maximiato," Dr. Johnson said, squatting in front of his chair. "I am to give you a physical examination. It is a final requirement of the law." He shook his head. "Don't ask me why."

Aba and Sister Ria said in unison, "No."

"You will not touch him," Sister Ria continued.

Johnson stood up and stepped back until he and Vargas were shoulder to shoulder. The physician ran his tongue over his lips and then nodded. "Looks healthy to me. Don Vargas?"

"To me as well," Vargas said softly. "Strong as a range bull . . . a great man of royal Spanish lineage."

The servants had brought chairs and trays of coffee and sweets, and Vargas and Johnson were sitting in front of Don Maximiato, talking about times past. Every so often Don Maximiato would nod, but he remained silent, gazing off toward the river and the distant fields beyond. Sister Ria stood holding his thin shoulders and looking down at him, something tearing loose in her chest, breaking up the last of her rigid stubbornness toward this man.

When they were ready to leave, Vargas motioned for Sister Ria to follow him. She patted her father's shoulder and joined Vargas on the other side of the buggy. He leaned into the carriage for support and handed her an envelope.

"What is it?" Her voice was cool.

"The papers for the sale."

She shook her head.

"Listen to me," he whispered. "It's only five acres. Take the money and repair La Cienega—do it, child." He stopped talking and looked across the darkness at his old friend sitting on the chair, Aba standing behind him. "You can't save him."

Sister Ria raised her eyebrows. "And what do you get if I sign it, Don Vargas?"

"Nothing," Vargas said, clearing his throat. "What did I call you as a child?"

She didn't answer him.

"Isadora," he said firmly.

"*La niña testaruda,*" she whispered.

"Yes. But you are no longer a child, Isadora." He shuffled his feet. "Your father will have no peace until you take control of La Cienega from him."

She shook her head slowly. "My father is mad."

Vargas studied her face. "Not completely, child. At times he is as sane as you. The day you returned, he told me to prepare—"

"I don't believe you," she interrupted.

The old man ignored the comment. "He told me to prepare the contract for the sale of La Brea and the title transfer of La Cienega to you. For his signature and yours." He held the papers out to her. "He has already signed, Isadora. I was not to give you these until after the execution. But I wanted you to know before he was gone." The old man watched her eyes. "Before it was too late for the two of you."

She was shaking her head again, tears running down her cheeks.

Don José climbed into the carriage and sat catching his breath. Then he looked down at her. "You had a dream once, Sister Ria." Her convent name sounded very formal now on his tongue.

She looked up and nodded.

"What was it?"

She wiped the dampness from her cheeks. "It's gone," she said.

Sister Ria opened the packet of papers Vargas had given her: The signature was her father's. Don Vargas and Reed Johnson had left over an hour ago, but she was still struggling to breathe. Aba and the other servants had gone inside, leaving her alone with her father. Earlier, she had seen Angel María standing in a window staring out at her. But the girl, too, was gone now.

She pulled up a chair close in front of him and grasped his hands in hers. He did not pull away; he just sat looking at her. She was fighting for control of her emotions. "Why?" she moaned. She waited for him to say something, but he just sat and watched her face. "What was I to you, Father? Property—like your horses and bulls? Tell me. What was I?" She waited a moment and then said, "Tell me that I am your daughter. Please."

He did not tell her.

She wiped her eyes on the sleeve of her habit and took a deep breath and patted his hand. "I'm sorry. It's too late for answers. I know that. Let me at least pray with you."

He shook his head.

She ignored him and moved her chair closer to him and began to pray. He did not resist. His hands were cold. She blew on them and rubbed them to warm them and prayed—prayed until she could no longer keep her eyes open. She leaned back in her chair and slipped into a deep, exhausted sleep.

When she awoke, little red bats were flitting around the eaves of the veranda, chasing insects near the lanterns. She was sitting in the rocking chair with a blanket draped over her. Aba must have put it there. Her father was gone. Fernando was sitting at her side, watching a large moth fluttering against the glass of a wall sconce. She felt a deep melancholy. Then she gasped: Her eyes locked on the moth. It was black, the margins of its wings wavy, with two large pink-rimmed spots that looked like eyes on its lower wings. It was the same creature she had smashed with the broom that night in the alley. She was certain of it.

She shivered and stood quickly, and the moth, as if sensing her intention, fluttered away into the night. Then it was suddenly back, circling her head in its unsteady flight, as if taunting her, and she was swinging wildly at it, the dark creature swirling in the mad eddies of her swings like a leaf caught in the fast waters of a stream. Then it was gone again.

She stood searching the porch and surrounding darkness for it, the house and grounds silent. She shivered and picked up the blanket from the tiles and pulled it over her shoulders. The bats continued their erratic flight under the eaves. The dark sky was speckled with a million stars. Slowly, she calmed down.

As she stood in the chill night, staring past the old stone fountain to the river and the distant fields, it was as if nothing had changed in her life. Yet everything had changed.

She went inside the house.

Fernando was trotting ahead of her down the darkened hallway when it happened. She never saw it coming. The hand shot out of the darkness and grabbed her throat.

The man was big. Too big to fight. Her only hope was escape. There was a brief moment of hesitancy before her years of combat with the town children came rushing back to her in a surprisingly quick reflex. She brought her knee up, slamming it hard into his groin. As soon as she delivered the blow, she shoved the man away and went down fast, sliding backward over the tiles. She froze, staring up at the policeman. His throat had been cut. He opened and shut his mouth, making a horrible sucking sound through the wide slit, and reached a hand out toward her. Then he shuddered and went down hard.

He was dead when she got to him.

Sister Ria crouched by the body, peering into the darkness. Nothing moved. Then she heard it. The sound was barely audible—the noise of furniture being moved, sliding into walls. Sister Ria tensed and stood probing the weak light with her eyes, listening for vibrations in the air, trying to understand. She started moving slowly toward the noise.

She had almost reached her room when she heard a muffled cry coming from inside. She lunged for the door.

The figure in the brown suit was bent over Estrella's cot, holding the girl pinned under the covers. Estrella was squealing, desperately struggling to get away, while Angel María stood and kicked at the intruder's legs. The figure whirled and slapped María hard across her face. She stumbled backward and fell at Sister Ria's feet.

"Leave her alone!" Sister Ria yelled.

The sheer volume of the scream caused the figure to step back from the bed into the darkness. Estrella came out from under the blankets, crying hysterically, "My hands are cut—"

Sister Ria grabbed both girls and shoved them out into the hallway. Estrella was still crying. "María, take Estrella and find Aba. Do not come back to this room. Do you understand?" The girl nodded. Sister Ria yanked the bedroom door shut, then whirled around. The figure had moved boldly back toward her. She tried to make out the face in the darkness but could not.

"She's just a child!" Sister Ria screamed. "You tried to kill a child!" Whatever natural fear Sister Ria had felt was replaced by wrath that surged up into her throat. "May God curse you!" She could see a knife blade in the darkness. "Put it down!"

But the figure did not put the knife down. Instead, it moved slowly toward her. That was all it took for Fernando. He leaped on the intruder's legs like a leopard. Suddenly, people were running and yelling in the hacienda, and the figure kicked free of the cat and darted through the door into the night, Sister Ria in pursuit.

They ran twisting and turning through the garden, matching each other stride for stride, locked in deadly silent maneuvering. Whenever the figure slowed, Sister Ria slowed, waiting for her chance, knowing she had to be careful of the knife. Then they were running again, dodging through the tangled maze of bushes.

They were deep in the garden and had stopped once more, Sister Ria on one side of a large bush, the figure out of sight on the other. She could hear the person panting in the darkness. Then silence. She held her breath and listened. Nothing. No sound except for the blood pounding in her.

Back inside the house, candles and lanterns were being lit in the upstairs rooms as the frantic search for the intruder continued. She edged around a tall, dense oleander bush, holding her breath and probing the night for movement on the other side, her fists clenched. Still nothing. Her fear told her to back away.

But she could not.

"Father?"

Silence.

She turned her head slowly back and forth, trying to pick up sound in the still night, listening for a twig breaking, a rustling of leaves. But there was nothing.

Sister Ria gathered her courage and lunged around the bush. No one.

Then she heard the screeching of the hinges.

The small door in the stone wall of the hacienda's foundation was open. She peered down the steps some fifteen feet into the root cellar, waiting at the dark opening until she got her bearings. The room below her was a large rectangle measuring forty by sixty feet. Its roof was the heavy bottom floor of the house, supported by a single line of large stone pillars running down the center at ten-foot intervals. She and Milagros had often played dolls in its cool shadows on hot summer days.

Sister Ria took a deep breath and held it. There were so many places to hide down there. Small rooms lined both sides of the long walls of the rectangle—rooms used for storing produce and jars of preserves for the hacienda's winter use; rooms where a person could be waiting. She let that breath go and quickly took another. There was a second door at the far end of the rectangle that opened out on the service road. But it was kept locked by Aba to prevent pilfering by the workers. Few knew where the key was hidden.

Sister Ria started down. She stumbled at the bottom of the steps, hesitated, and then forced herself to scramble through the pitch blackness of the storage rooms on one side of the cellar. Her breath heaved. These rooms were empty. She was just starting to cross to the other side to check the rooms there when she heard the sound of something moving in the darkness. Then it was still again. She trembled and wanted to turn and flee but could not.

She pulled herself up straight and squared her shoulders. The person was standing in the shadows somewhere nearby. Instinctively, she moved through the black gloom until she touched the heavy stone pillar in the center of the room, backing up against it for protection. She held her breath and opened her mouth slightly and listened again. She jumped. Off to her right, a jar had fallen, shattering on the floor. Frightened, she pressed harder into the stones of the pillar and waited.

Then she heard the whisper. It hissed at her, mocking her: "Holy Sister—please help me. Please." It was the voice she had heard in the alley, the voice from outside her garden door. Anger rose, burning in her throat.

"Go to hell!" she shouted.

The room fell silent again.

Long minutes passed before she felt, more than heard, another movement and canted her head toward it. Something was stirring in the darkness. There was a small window high up the wall opposite her, and a soft beam of moonlight spilled in onto the floor. Again she heard a sound. Closer this time. She balled her fists. Then she saw a large dark shape dart across the light, and she sucked all the air she could into her lungs. Ready to fight.

Sister Ria was trying to hear, or see, or sense something that would tell her where the figure had gone. Should she move? No, that would give away her position. As she was worrying through these thoughts, the sickening realization came to her: She was now alone in the cellar. The figure had escaped out the second door.

"No!" she cried.

She whirled and desperately felt with her hands over the cold surface of the heavy pillar: The small stone near the top was missing. She was gasping for breath. Aba kept the key behind that stone. She began to pound on the rocks of the pillar, a long, low, wailing sob coming from someplace deep inside her. The key was gone.

Frantically, she retraced her steps, knocking over baskets of produce, falling and getting up and running again, bounding up the stairs, back out into the night and the garden. Once in the open, she broke into a hard run. She went past the stone gazebo, up the wide flight of marble stairs, down a narrow passageway behind the work sheds, and slid to a stop. The second door was still shut. Her heart was pounding in her ears. It was all she could hear now.

She rocked back and forth on her feet; her fists, still covered with the policeman's blood, were clenching and unclenching. She stiffened with grim determination when she heard the key turn in the rusty lock. What seemed like an eternity passed before the small rear door to the root cellar slowly opened and the figure in the brown suit stepped out into the night.

"Why?" Sister Ria said.

The figure jumped slightly at the sound of her voice.

"Why?" Sister Ria repeated, the word more a moan than a question.

The figure in the brown suit was holding a small derringer in one hand. Sister Ria did not care. She stepped closer. "Why?"

The figure reached up and yanked off the fedora and sailed it into the night. Milagros's lustrous black hair fell over her shoulders. "What don't you understand, little sister?"

"None of it."

Milagros's eyes narrowed. "You have been in the convent too long."

"That's not an answer!"

"You want an answer?" Milagros hissed. "I'll give you one. Two years ago my husband threw me out so that he could move a god-damned prostitute into my house! Can you understand that?" She gave a mirthless laugh. "I was tossed out onto the streets of San Francisco with nothing. Nothing."

Sister Ria watched her.

"He threw me out so he could move in a whore. I was a Mexican divorcée in the Anglo city of San Francisco. Do you know what that means?" She was shaking her head and breathing hard. Sister Ria did not answer. "No, I didn't think you did. It means I might as well have been dead."

Sister Ria pressed her palms together and closed her eyes.

"Don't give me your damn prayers, Isadora."

Sister Ria ignored her.

"I had nothing, so I turned to our beloved father. You know him, the father who tried to turn you into a man."

Sister Ria continued praying.

"Look at me, dammit!"

Sister Ria opened her eyes with her palms still pressed together in front of her face. When she spoke, her voice was low and firm. "Millie, you killed a woman and her baby. You killed the policeman. You tried to kill Estrella. Millie, what's wrong with you?"

"I don't want your morality."

Aba was calling Sister Ria's name in the distance.

Milagros paced back and forth in front of her. "You know what our dear father said when I asked for help? He said: 'You married a Yankee *perro*. So live with the dogs.'" She waved an arm at the darkness. "He wouldn't even welcome me back to this: a house of mud, life as an old maid, life with that bitch of a servant. He did me a favor." Her voice was laced with disdain. "I wouldn't have come back even if he had begged me—not back to the same two-bit pueblo that I ran from. That you ran from, don't you forget." Milagros shook her head. "No, I wasn't coming back. No matter what, I wasn't coming back." Her voice drifted off.

"Millie, why, why? Why have you done these things?"

Milagros ignored the question and laughed. "Home to all this splendor. I asked him for money, he gave me nothing."

Sister Ria just stared at her sister.

"I asked him for a thousand dollars a month, and he gave me nothing."

"He has almost nothing, Millie."

Milagros focused on her sister. "I'm not a fool, Izzie. I know that," she snapped, unbuttoning the brown cutaway jacket. "He deserves what he got."

"Oh, Millie—"

Milagros cut her off. "I don't want your religion, I don't want your pity!" Her lovely face was distorted with a wild anger. "You asked why, and so I'm telling you! That's all." She caught her breath and then continued, "When the gas company wanted La Brea, I begged him to sell."

Sister Ria's voice sounded distant. "So he could pay you money."

"I was desperate! I was his daughter, I had put up with his madness for all those years—he owed me that!"

"Why, Millie? Why?"

"Don't play stupid, Izzie. You were always good at that—believing that dear old sweet God was going to come off His heavenly perch and make everything right in our lives. Well, He didn't, did He?" Millie frowned darkly. "I learned when we were kids that the only things I could count on were the things I took myself." She smiled an odd smile, twisting her features into a strange masklike expression that made Sister Ria shiver. "So I killed the whore because I knew a Mexican killing an American woman—whore or not—was going away for life. And I left his things in her room, certain the cretins they call police in this town would arrest him. And I was just as certain he would act like a madman and get himself convicted."

"He is our father," Sister Ria moaned.

"Don't pull your righteousness with me, Isadora. I stood up for you with him too many times for you to pull that on me!"

"Why?" Sister Ria sobbed.

"Because once he was gone, I was going to own this grand pile of mud." Milagros continued to pace. "He likes playacting, and he played this one superbly. Only he played it too well, and they condemned him to death. That was his doing, not mine."

Sister Ria shuddered, unable to speak.

"I knew the court would award La Cienega to us." Milagros

laughed and looked at her sister. "And I never thought you'd come back."

"She was going to have a child."

"A bastard, you mean?"

Sister Ria was not listening. She was gazing into the shadows on the ground, remembering the times when they had played dolls with their nursemaids, collected shells along the beach, raced their ponies, fished for crawdads in the river. Her heart had never left those days. She looked up slowly at Milagros, focusing on her sister's face. Her words, when she found her voice, were woven with deep sorrow. "You thought it was me in the bed tonight. Didn't you, Millie? You thought it was me, and you were going to kill me."

Milagros did not hesitate. "Yes."

Sister Ria closed her eyes.

"Yes," Milagros repeated.

"Oh, Millie—"

"You did this to yourself," Milagros said. "I told you to leave." She pulled off the brown suit jacket and tossed it on the ground. "I tried to scare you off by killing that stupid chicken and placing the dead bastard child in the manger and all the rest. But Your Holiness had to stay and meddle." She paused. "And then I realized that you were just like him—stubborn. I was right, wasn't I?" Milagros was shaking her head, her dark hair flying in the night air. "So don't you blame me. You brought this on yourself."

The realization came over Sister Ria suddenly. Her sister had inherited her father's madness. Only Milagros's was far worse than his:

It was laced with the impulse to murder. Sister Ria pulled herself up to her full height and asked, "How many?"

"How many what?"

"How many people have you killed?"

Millie turned her head slightly and listened to the sound of the searchers at the house, ignoring the question. "You brought this on yourself, Izzie."

"Just tell me how many."

Millie didn't answer.

"You killed Ruperto Tristan, didn't you? And Elsie. You drowned poor little Emilia. How many, Millie, have there been?"

Milagros stared off into the night for a moment, then looked back at her sister and said, "It doesn't matter."

"It matters. You're ill, Millie."

"I'm not crazy! Ruperto Tristan was going to take you away, leaving me behind in this place."

"And Elsie—what did she do?"

Milagros laughed derisively. "Don't joke with me. That little trollop would have become the doña; we would have had a fifteen-year-old mother. I wasn't going to let that happen."

"Millie, she was going to run away! We planned it with her, you and I planned it." Sister Ria studied her sister's face. "How many more, Millie?"

"I don't know how many!" Milagros screamed. "It doesn't matter! He would have just brought Elsie back," she whispered.

Sister Ria's voice sounded distant even to herself. "When I was a child, you stood up for me. And you were just a child yourself, but so very brave. And I loved you."

"That doesn't matter, either, now."

"Yes, it does, Millie. It will always matter." She sighed deeply. "Oh, Millie, why?"

Milagros cocked the hammer on the little pistol. "Turn around, Izzie."

"No." Sister Ria inhaled a deep breath. "You'll see my face. You'll see what we once were to each other." She stopped talking and then added, "I won't turn."

"Turn," Milagros snapped.

Sister Ria was crying. She made a sweeping gesture with her hand and bowed at the waist. "I present the Grand La Conquistadora. She fears nothing." When she straightened up, Milagros was pointing the pistol at her.

"That was a child's game, Izzie."

"It was our game. Before you became sick, Millie. What we believed. *Ruegue para su alma*—pray for her soul."

"He wouldn't help me," Milagros moaned. "I tried to get work. But I don't know how to work. The only thing I could do was clean people's houses. That's all." She stared at Sister Ria's face. "I cleaned houses for two years. I washed floors and rich Americans' filthy undergarments. And they treated me like trash. I couldn't do that anymore, Izzie. I couldn't. You understand."

"I don't."

"Turn around, Izzie."

Sister Ria broke a rose from a nearby bush and tossed it at Mila-gros's feet. "Take it with you when you're done. La Rosa de Castilla. To remember us." Milagros looked down briefly at the rose, then up at her sister's face. For an instant, her features seemed to soften, and Sister Ria thought she looked like La Conquistadora once again. Millie raised her hand to her head. Seconds later, the shot from Mil-lie's derringer blew the hair out on one side of her head, like a small puff of wind.

Sister Ria knelt and put her hand over Millie's heart and then to the side of her throat. There was still a faint beating, but the small dark hole at the side of the head told her it would soon stop. She held Millie tight against her chest, whispering into her ear while there was still time, remembering for her their lives together when they were children—their days at the seashore, the hundreds of games they'd played, the thousand nights they'd read in bed to-gether—telling her how much she loved her, reminding her that she had once been loyal and brave and good, that once she had not been sick.

Then Millie shuddered and was gone.

Sister Ria held her for a long time in the darkness, talking qui-etly to her. When she was finally done, she placed the rose in Millie's hand and kissed her cheek. "*Ruegue para su alma,*" she whispered.

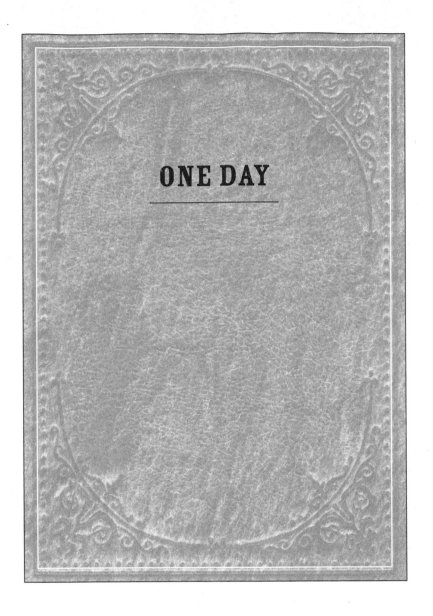

ONE DAY

CHAPTER 19

THE MEXICAN PART of Los Angeles was a dusty shade of taupe, but there were green places, and Sister Ria was sitting on a bench near the old pueblo fountain gazing at one: the tendrils of an ancient creeper that spread over an adobe wall like the thick fingers of a moss-colored hand. She was staring as if she could see people moving in the vine, remembering her sister, and praying for forgiveness for both their souls. Her thoughts drifted to Fernando. The old cat had not been seen since Milagros had kicked him in the bedroom. Sister Ria said a prayer for him as well.

She stirred. Don José Vargas's servant Antonio Mollena was hurrying up the road toward her, holding out an envelope. "Señora. Don Vargas has spoken to the governor."

"Thank you."

The man dipped his head and walked quickly away. Vargas had left on the morning train for Sacramento to see the American governor and tell him there was proof of Don Maximiato's innocence.

She ran a finger under the envelope's flap. *Doña Isadora: Don Maximiato's journey of death will continue. Vargas.*

✝

Sister Ria and Aba were marching shoulder to shoulder down the loggia of the hacienda, headed for Don Maximiato's room, when they saw the children. Min, Estrella, Cristina, and the orphans in their new shoes, all of them were standing in two long lines against both walls of the wide hallway. Angel María was standing at the end of one line. When Sister Ria looked at her, Angel turned around and stared out a window. They were all crying. Estrella stepped forward. She held a large tin pail stuffed with roses in her bandaged hands. "For the patrón." She sniffed. "We each picked one."

"Thank you, children," Sister Ria said. "They will make him very happy."

Estrella brought the back of her hand to her mouth and started to sob.

"Hush," Aba said sternly, "you all have work to do. Min, make certain the children do their work. I will inspect it later."

"Have any of you seen Fernando?" Sister Ria asked. The children shook their heads and sobbed louder.

"Min," Aba snapped. "I will inspect their work later."

The two women started off down the hall again, turning a corner and approaching a young policeman Hood had posted that morning at the patrón's bedroom door. Two others were stationed on the front veranda. The young man jumped up and yanked off his cap when he saw the women. Then he looked at Sister Ria, dressed in her stark black-and-white habit, and quickly crossed himself. "Ladies," he said in a voice that broke into a squeak, "my orders are to check you for weapons."

Sister Ria stopped. Aba did not. The old woman grabbed Sister Ria by the arm and marched her around the boyish-looking police-man.

"You will check nothing," Aba snapped, "you are a guest in the house of the patrón."

"Yes, ma'am," the young man mumbled.

Don Maximiato was sitting in the center of his bedroom, paint-ing at his easel. He was dressed in a bright red toreador's outfit—the sequins reflecting the lamplight as though they were scales on a large red fish—his spindly calves covered in gauzy white stockings, black slippers on his feet. As he had been the previous night on the ve-randa, he was working fast.

Sister Ria stepped behind him and put a hand on his shoulder. "Father, it is Isadora."

"No," he snapped.

He was painting what looked like a woman, the body clothed in a dark dress, the head not yet brushed onto the canvas. She leaned close to him and whispered, "I am your daughter." Her voice broke with emotion. "Please say that."

He continued painting.

She pulled a stool close to him and sat and took a deep breath. "Surely you remember our life together." She began to tell him everything she could remember about their lives. Big and small things, good things: about how the great horse Bisonte had saved her, about the mornings when they had sat together in the cafés drinking coffee and arguing with the old men of the pueblo about the world and life. She told him about her mother and brother, about Milagros as a girl. She did not tell him about Milagros's death or what Milagros had done. She would let God do that. She told him how proud she had been when he bought the children shoes and when he had buried Dorothy Regal's child. She remembered for him the day he had painted her on the beach. She told him that she still had the painting, would keep it always.

She talked to him for over two hours. Don Maximiato continued to work. But she sensed he was listening. She took the brush gently from his hand and turned him on his stool so that he was facing her. She grasped both of his hands, cleared her throat, and said, "I am your daughter—please at least say that."

He looked at her face, and their eyes held for a moment. Then he turned back to the easel and swirled a brush in a can of thinner and wiped it clean on a rag and said nothing.

"Father—" she said, her voice breaking.

"Can you not see that I am working?"

Sister Ria wiped at her eyes and smiled. "Yes, Father."

It was done.

He went back to his painting. Sister Ria went to Aba. "I have said what I wanted to say," she whispered, "now you must."

Aba shook her head, and Sister Ria could see that the old

woman was worrying her hands. "You must do it now," Sister Ria hissed.

"*Silencio!*" he snapped, dabbing his brush in a gob of green paint on his mixing board.

Sister Ria looked at Aba, raised her eyebrows, and nodded fiercely in the direction of her father. The old woman walked slowly toward him.

Sister Ria was moving to the back of the room to give Aba privacy when she saw it. The door to the small room was cracked open a few inches. She heard Aba say his name, and she pushed the door open and stepped inside, closing it behind her. No light was burning in this room, but there was a small oval window at one end that let in the sun's light. The compartment was a small rectangle, some twelve feet by twenty.

Sister Ria let her eyes adjust to the shadows, trying not to listen to the muffled sound of Aba's voice. Her eyes scanned the walls of the room. Suddenly, she wanted to sit down.

It was a gallery of his paintings.

They hung on the walls, covering every inch of space. Stacks of other canvases leaned against the walls. Hundreds of them. But that was not what caused her to stand with her mouth open. It was the paintings themselves. It was as if the Lugo family had come alive around her. There were pictures of her mother, Milagros, Ramón, and her. Dozens of paintings. Paintings of her and her siblings at different ages, from babies, to youngsters, to young adults.

Sister Ria pressed her hands to her mouth. She had never seen any of these, had never seen him working on any of them. He had carefully observed his children and wife, made mental notes about coloring and moods, then retired to the solitude of his room to paint them into liquid life. They were wonderful paintings, capturing individual moods and personalities. Most amazing of all, this man who had such a difficult time relating to his family had painted himself into each canvas in close, loving poses—an arm around a shoulder, a hand on an arm, gazing proudly at his children, his smiling face haunting the shadowy background of a portrait. There was a picture of Milagros as a young girl, before the illness had taken her. Sister Ria reached up and gently touched the face in the picture. *"Ruegue para su alma,"* she whispered.

Then her eyes locked on a picture of herself as a young child sitting at the library table. She had been reading, unaware that he was standing in a doorway behind her, gazing fondly at her. She began to cry.

When she had gotten control of her emotions, she looked up at another painting of herself as a child of eleven or twelve, her father's arm around her shoulder. They were both smiling. Sister Ria took it from the wall.

She opened the door and walked out into the room. He was still working at his easel. Aba nodded at her. Sister Ria returned the nod and, clutching the painting against her breast, walked over and put a hand to her father's cheek. He didn't react.

She studied his face for a long time. Finally, she drew in a sharp breath and held the painting out in front of him. "Father, who is that?" She pointed at the child in the picture. "Who? Tell me!"

He said nothing. Sister Ria looked down at the top of his head, wiping the tears from her cheeks.

When she was convinced he would not respond, she said, "I had a dream once—but I set it aside for God. So I know how hard it was for you." She felt him tense, and his brush hesitated over the canvas. But then he was back painting again. She cleared her throat and said, "I'm sorry you didn't live your dream."

He said nothing.

She had turned and was walking slowly toward the door when she heard it. "Daughter—" he mumbled. It felt as if God had touched her, as He had that day so long ago in the sea. The hatred and mistrust were gone. She turned and stared at him. He was still painting.

"Thank you," she said.

That was when she made her decision. She set the painting down and pulled the papers that Don José Vargas had given her the night before from her pocket and signed them in front of her father. He continued painting, but she knew he was also watching her. She said, "There is one more thing we need to do, Father."

✝

The young policeman jumped up from his chair and backed away nervously as the old woman and the nun marched out of Don Maximiato's room and down the loggia. "Have a good evening, ladies," he called. Neither of them turned around. He shrugged.

✝

Chief Raymond Hood, determined to avoid trouble with the crowds of Mexicans gathering on the road to La Cienega, had come early with his deputies, entering the patrón's bedroom at three-thirty A.M. It was dark and chilly.

Don Maximiato was sitting alone in front of his easel, staring at the fresh canvas, as a deputy cuffed his hands behind him. Hood looked at the painting and shook his head. The man had painted his old servant, making her look almost special.

"Morning, Max," Hood said. The patrón ignored him. "You ready, Rojo?" Hood yelled out the door.

The young newspaper editor had been hired by the sheriff to photograph the proceedings, purportedly to document things. But Clemente Rojo figured it was as much an election ploy on the part of the police chief. Even so, he would do it and run the photos in *La Verdad.* He had photographed the original murder scene, when Don Maximiato was arrested, the trial, the jury, Don Maximiato convicted, and now he would photograph the execution. To honor the man.

"Rojo!"

"Yes, I'm ready."

"Good." Hood turned and looked at Don Maximiato. "You want a cigarette?"

Don Maximiato shook his head.

"You want to write anything?"

He did not respond. Hood stood looking down at him, thinking that the man was dressed appropriately: black boots, black pants, a waist-length black cape, a black silk scarf wound around his neck and up over half his face against the chill, and a black gaucho hat pulled low.

"Dammit, Rojo, let's get this going," Hood said.

The editor ignored him and respectfully took off his hat and said in Spanish, "May God bless and keep you, Don Maximiato."

Don Maximiato said nothing.

"Let's get on with it," Hood barked. The police chief turned back to the patrón. "Well, I guess this is the end of the fiesta, Don. We thought we'd get a good photograph of you and me together."

Hood adjusted his bow tie and quickly combed his silver hair. Then he waited until Rojo was ready. When the editor nodded at him, the chief of police turned and pulled Don Maximiato's scarf off and stood staring openmouthed into the nun's beautiful face. Sister Ria was looking past the sheriff to the bedroom door where Angel María stood holding Fernando in her arms.

Angel and Sister Ria both smiled.

The photograph was excellent.

Out in the bay of San Pedro lay a ship with her sails unfurled. The morning was still dark, but a thin strip of pink was etching the tops of the San Gabriel Mountains east of Los Angeles. All but two of the people on deck were sailors. The ship's captain, a weathered-looking Irishman with silver hair and a long-stemmed pipe in his mouth, was standing beside these two.

Aba was gazing toward the land. "How long will it take?" she asked.

"This time of year, with stops in Buenos Aires and Havana, I'd say we'll make Spain in seven weeks."

The nun standing next to Aba was chain-smoking cigarettes and looking with an appraising eye at the captain's clothing. Unable to contain himself any longer, the nun sidled up next to the man and said, "I like your hat, Captain."

The captain looked down at the nun, who had a three-day growth of stubble on his chin, and said, "Thanks."

The nun cleared his throat, took a quick draw on his cigarette, leaned closer to the captain, and whispered, "I'm not really a nun."

"I guessed that."

"I'm a painter. And I'm going to Sevilla to paint sunsets." He gave the captain's hat another long, appraising look and asked, "Do you like this outfit I'm wearing?"

"Don Maximiato, it is time for your rest," Aba said, taking the old man's arm and walking him down the deck. He pulled away and moved to the ship's rail and stared across the waters at the dark shoreline. He studied it for a time before he asked, "La Cienega and the children?"

"You know the answer, Don Maximiato."

"Tell me again."

"Isadora will restore La Cienega."

"And the children?"

"She will care for them. She will turn the hacienda into a grand home for castaways. Children were her dream."

He smiled.

The wind was picking up.

ACKNOWLEDGMENTS

I want to thank my editor, Laura Ford, for all of her hard and diligent work. She put up with my writer's whims with admirable grace and perseverance.

Barney Karpfinger is a friend and a fine literary agent. He carefully guided me through the publishing forest with a combination of hardheadedness and uncommonly good commonsense.

ABOUT THE AUTHOR

THOMAS EIDSON is the acclaimed author of *The Missing*, which
was made into a major motion picture directed
by Ron Howard, *St. Agnes' Stand, All God's Children,* and *Hannah's Gift*.
He lives in Marblehead, Massachusetts.

ABOUT THE TYPE

This book was set in Requiem, a typeface designed by the
Hoefler Type Foundry. It is a modern typeface inspired by
inscriptional capitals in Ludovico Vicentino degli Arrighi's 1523
writing manual, *Il modo de temperare le penne*. An original lowercase,
a set of figures, and an italic in the "chancery" style that Arrighi
helped popularize were created to make this adaptation of
a classical design into a complete font family.